A Fly Named Alfred

A Fly Named Alfred

Don Trembath

ORCA BOOK PUBLISHERS

Canadian Cataloguing in Publication Data

Trembath, Don, 1963 –
    A fly named Alfred

    ISBN 1-55143-083-5

    I. Title.
PS8589.R392F59 1997   jC813'.54 C96–910828–1
PZ7.T71925F1 1997

Library of Congress Catalog Card Number: 97-65299

Orca Book Publishers gratefully acknowledges the support of our
publishing programs provided by the following agencies: the
Department of Canadian Heritage, The Canada Council for the Arts,
and the British Columbia Ministry of Small Business, Tourism and
Culture.

Cover design by Christine Toller
Cover illustration by Ron Lightburn/Limner Imagery

Printed and bound in Canada

Orca Book Publishers   **Orca Book Publishers**
PO Box 5626, Station B   PO Box 468
Victoria, BC V8R 6S4   Custer, WA 98240-0468
Canada   USA

97 98 99   5 4 3 2

To Billy and Harper
and all the other characters in my world.

< 1 >

You want to hear something funny? I'll tell you.

I was sitting in the library, minding my own business, for a change, when Trevor Carson and Tommy Rowe walk in with a copy of the school newspaper. It's called *Ragtime* — for good reason, too, if you ask me. The thing is laid out like a tabloid, but the pictures in it never turn out, and the stories go on forever. I mean, two weeks ago, the editorial was continued on three different pages.

Anyway, they walk in and sit down practically right beside me and they just get the paper open when Veronica MacLeish and Cindy Charles, the two most beautiful girls in the history of high school, walk in and join them. The four of them sitting there reminded me of one of those hair commercials you see on television all the time, or gum commercials, where everybody is laughing and smiling and never saying anything because no one can remember their lines.

In this one, you have the fabulously beautiful Veronica swooshing her long black hair in everyone's face, and the lovely and talented Cindy with the short brown hair and the ultra-cool glasses with the wire frames that everyone must comment on or else she cries, and the overgrown, under-brained Tommy, with his crewcut and a tattoo of a shark on his arm, and the short, stocky, curly-haired, "don't-call-me-fat-or-I'll-eat-your-face" Trevor.

They all say hi to each other and giggle and talk about how boring Social Studies is. Of course, they don't even look at me. Then they open the paper to page five and start reading the column called "Fly On The Wall." It's a regular feature in the paper written by this guy who observes people all the time and then writes about them. It's like that saying you hear people use all the time, "I'd like to be a fly on the wall in that meeting, or class, or whatever."

Well, the guy who writes the column is a fly on the wall.

This week the column is about a student who walks into the cafeteria and buys a Coke. The student pops open the Coke, takes a huge swig, belches, takes another huge swig, belches again, then flips the empty can into the recycling bin and walks out.

The column goes,

I don't know what he enjoyed more, the Coke or the belches, or what he needed more, the Coke or the belches, but he was sure contented when he left the cafeteria.

I suppose you could say he was taking care of himself, or doing what he had to do to relax and get through the rest of the day.

Some people do this with tea and a cookie, or

*milk and a candy bar, or coffee and a cigarette. I
guess now we can add Coke and a belch to the list.
It is not quite as soothing as the others, but you
won't die from it, and you'll never have to worry
about anyone bothering you. In fact, if privacy is a
concern, I would recommend it.*

*This guy could clear out a room faster than a
fire alarm. He's about as loud as one, too.*

The fantastic foursome sitting at my table took about
ten minutes to read it, even though it is only about two
hundred words long, but when they finished, they were
laughing their heads off.

"This kills me every time," said Trevor.

I wish.

"Old Alfred," said Tommy, still looking at the paper
and laughing. The column is written by someone named
Alfred, but no one believes that Alfred is his real name.
"You're a cool guy, Alfred. I wish I knew who you were
so I could tell you in person."

Then he looked up and saw me staring at him.

"What are you looking at, Winslow?" he said. All
signs of laughter and good humor disappeared from his
face.

"Nothing," I said.

"Yes, you are. What are you looking at?"

Now you tell me, why do people ask a question like
that twice in a row? As if I'm going to come clean and
say to him, "Honestly, Tom, you want to know what I'm
looking at? You really want to know? I'm looking at
you, you big, greasy ape, and I'm wondering how you

got your T-shirt over your thick head, and how you managed to walk all the way from math class to here with gum in your mouth without tripping."

"I'm not looking at anything," I said. "I'm just doing my math."

"Hey, do mine when you're done," said Trevor.

"I don't know how to do this," I said. I wasn't kidding either. Math isn't exactly my favorite subject in the world, and I have the grades to prove it.

"Well, figure it out," said Trevor.

"Yeah, figure it out," said Tommy. He was standing up all of a sudden. "Now let's see what you got in your lunch." He's a pretty big guy, like I said. He could probably eat about three lunches and still have room for a snack before supper.

He grabbed my lunch bag before I could get it and pulled out the sandwiches and cookies my mom had made. Naturally, the cookies were cut in the shape of hearts and had little red sprinkles on them. I was with my mom in the kitchen when she was making them and I told her, "Mom, please don't do that to all the cookies. You know somebody at school is going to see them."

"Are you afraid they might get jealous and ask you for one?" she said. She's so proud of her cookies.

"No, Mom. That's not what I'm afraid of," I said.

"Aww, isn't this cute?" said Tommy. "Little Harper's mommy gives him little cookies with little red sprinkles on top. Aww."

"Those look good," said Cindy, who also happens to be one of the biggest witches in the history of high school, along with her friend Veronica. "Give me one."

"Sure," said Tommy. "One for you."

He started handing out the cookies, but there were only four of them, so you can guess how many I got. Then he looked back in my lunch bag.

"Anyone want an apple?"

"No."

"No."

"No."

"Carrot stick?"

"No."

"No."

"I'll have one," said Veronica. "I love carrots. They're good for my hair." She ran her fingers through her hair as she said it. She wears about a thousand rings on her fingers, so I was surprised they didn't get all caught up or snagged on something. That would have been a story for the paper — Girl Ties Self Up With Hair, Friends Flee From Smelly Underarms.

He gave her the carrot sticks.

"Hear that, Winslow? Veronica here loves carrots. So you know what? Why don't you bring her carrot sticks every day so she doesn't have to worry about going without them?"

"I want more of those cookies," said Cindy.

"And you can bring Cindy some more of those cookies."

"I could use some extra cash," said Trevor. He was nodding his curly little head up and down as he talked, as if he had given the matter some serious thought, which was practically impossible, given that he played football and all, and had come up with this for an answer.

"And you can bring Trevor some extra cash. I'm sure you got enough to spare. Now let's see what I want. Hmmm. I'll have to think. Let me see. No, nothing's coming to me. I'll have to let you know, okay? Don't run away now. When I figure out what I want, I'll want it right away. I don't want to go looking for you. You stay right here where we can find you."

I nodded and picked up my empty lunch bag from the floor. Like I was really going to bring extra carrots, cookies, and money for these bozos.

Tommy stood up and said, "Bye-bye, Winslow, and thanks for lunch. Tell your mom to put a little more meat in the sandwiches next time. No wonder you're so skinny."

They were laughing like crazy when they left.

I had five bucks from my allowance in my pocket, so I knew I wouldn't have to go the rest of the day without food. But you know, I really wasn't that hungry all of a sudden. I guess that's what happens when somebody just comes in and takes everything that belongs to you and leaves again.

I left the library a few minutes later and hung out at my locker and read a book during lunch. Then I went to Biology, where some days I actually envy the insects we're dissecting. That's how boring Biology is. Then I went to English, which was my last class of the day.

Veronica was already there. She's in my class. She was yapping away to her little circle of friends and didn't even say anything about my lunch or the carrot sticks. I thought maybe she would say something. You know how people are when they're alone compared to when they're in a group? Sometimes they feel bad about something they've done and they want to apologize. But not her. She was telling everybody about the big fast car her boyfriend was picking her up in after school.

Of course, that made her the coolest person in the world.

Veronica's boyfriend doesn't go to our school. He's eighteen and has a job somewhere and is thinking about getting his own place. She made sure she told everyone that about a thousand times before class started.

When English finally ended, I went to my locker and put a few things in my book bag and then went outside. I was walking home, so I didn't stand with everyone else where the school buses pull in, but today the buses couldn't pull in because there was this shiny blue convertible parked crossways in the bus lane.

Practically the entire student body was standing there looking at the thing. Actually, they were looking at the guy in the car who was yelling at the bus drivers to go park somewhere else. He was here first, he was saying. The bus drivers were telling him to move it or they'd drive right over him. He didn't like hearing that very much. He stood up in the car, jumped over the windshield so he was on the hood, ripped off his shirt, and dared all of them to run over him.

Then the principal, Mr. Jenkins, came out and tried to settle everything down. Everybody booed him. Mr. Jenkins is not the most popular person in the school.

Then Veronica came out and hopped into the car on the passenger's side and just sat there trying to look serious, as if this was something gravely important going on, and she didn't care if there was one person watching or three hundred.

I guess this was the boyfriend she was talking about. He was tall and lean and had long stringy blond hair and these sunglasses on that wrapped halfway around his head. He was pretty wild-looking, if you ask me. He kept going on with his act on the hood of his car for another few minutes. He was really getting into it with Mr. Cunneyworth, one of the bus drivers. He was calling Mr. Cunneyworth an old man and telling him to get back in his bus before he got hurt.

Mr. Cunneyworth happens to be a pretty big man, like about six-foot three and way over two hundred pounds, and he was wearing this grey bus driver's uniform that was a bit small on him, making him look even bigger. All he said was, "Is that a fact?" and stood in front of the car with his arms crossed in front of his chest. He was wearing sunglasses, too. Those aviator sunglasses that pilots wear. But Mr. Cunneyworth did not look like a pilot. He looked more like a drill sergeant preparing to take his boys to war. And he didn't look too worried about going either.

Finally Veronica stood up in her seat and said something to her boyfriend that got him back in the car. He backed the thing away from Mr. Cunneyworth, then roared past him and everybody else at about two hundred miles an hour.

Everybody booed Mr. Cunneyworth, then they got out their bus passes and waited for their bus to pull up.

That was my drama for the day, I guess.

When I got home I made myself a sandwich and

watched a little TV. My mom and dad were out — surprise, surprise — so I was home alone.

Mom and Dad are out a lot, in case you were wondering.

Ironically, usually on a Tuesday I would be out, too, at this writing class I've been taking, but it doesn't start for another few weeks.

So anyway, after my sandwich I took Herbie, this poodle my parents bought me last summer, for a walk. He did his usual routine of sniffing every square inch of the path we take to the store and back. He's such a mutt.

Sometimes on Sundays, Mom and Dad and Herbie and I pile into the car and go for a walk somewhere in the city. Herbie loves it when we all go together because he gets about fifty times more hugs and kisses than when it's just me.

I like those days myself, if you want to know the truth.

This one time, these kids were playing this baseball game where one kid hits the ball and the other kids try to catch it, and Dad decided that it was time to show us what a fantastic baseball player he still is, or was, or whatever. So he asked the kid with the bat if he could have a turn, and the kid said sure, and Dad took the bat and tossed the ball in the air and took this huge swing at it and knocked it right in the middle of the lake that was about a mile to the left of where all the kids were standing waiting to catch the ball.

Naturally Mom and I gave him a standing ovation. But he still had to get the ball, so he went over to Herbie, who sometimes likes the water and other times wants nothing to do with it, and said, "Come on, boy. Let's go get the ball. Come on." And Herbie looked at him and tipped his head to the side the way dogs do when they think their owners have completely lost their minds, and laid down on the grass and went to sleep.

Dad ended up renting a paddle boat for ten bucks and paddling out to get the kids their ball.

When we got back home, and after I chased Herbie around the backyard fo a while, I did a little bit of homework and some other stuff and read this book I was reading.

A couple of weeks later the next edition of *Ragtime* came out and, much to my surprise, I discovered that old Alfred had written about Veronica and her boyfriend and their shiny blue convertible. His column went like this:

> *Maybe they were pretending to be Bonnie and Clyde, but if you ask me, they came off looking more like Elvis and Priscilla.*
>
> *I mean, he was doing a song and dance number on the hood of his car, he had the legs going and the whole bit, and she was his loyal supporter, sitting in the passenger seat, looking pretty, fully aware of the attention they were getting.*
>
> *They seemed to be, from their appearance, a few years apart in age too, he being the older one.*
>
> *It all makes me wonder if they were zooming off to Graceland when they left. That would be a logical place to go.*

Maybe that's what she said to him when she leaned over the windshield of his car. She said, "Honey, let's go to Graceland," and he said, "You little hound dog, you read ma mind."

Let's hope that's what she said.

One performance like that in a lifetime is enough.

I thought it was hilarious. I read it in the library after my math class. It kind of made my day, if you know what I mean. I mean, it's nice when someone else gets made fun of once in a while.

Anyway, I was just getting my math books out to do my homework when Tommy Rowe walked in and he came straight over to me. He didn't even look to see if there was anyone else in the library.

"Get up," he said. He sounded like a gangster. I'm surprised he didn't have his hand in his pocket, pretending it was a gun. Not that he needed one. The shark on his forearm was usually enough to get me going. People with tattoos make me nervous.

"What?"

"Get up and come with me," he said.

"I'm doing my math," I said. Nervous or not, I didn't feel like going with him to do some dumb thing that he wanted me to do.

But then he put one of his big shovel-hands on my math book so I couldn't open it and he glared into my eyes with a look that made me forget how to add two plus two. He was pretty mad about something.

"Get up and come with me," he said, this time very

controlled, between clenched teeth.

I decided that maybe I would like to do something dumb that he wanted me to do.

We went out into the hallway, then down the hall to the stairs, up the stairs and down the hall to the mezzanine overlooking the gym, then through the mezzanine and into the weight room. It was empty. He told me to sit down on one of the benches. He remained standing.

"Okay," he said. He started pacing back and forth, like he was nervous or something. It was all very strange. "Remember the other day, in the library, when I told you I had to think about what I wanted from you?"

"I thought you were joking," I said.

He stopped walking and looked me in the eye. "I don't joke," he said.

I half-expected to hear music in the background, like the kind you hear in those old gangster movies.

"Oh. I didn't know that," I said.

"Well, now you do. Anyway, I asked you a question. Do you remember the day I told you I had to think about what I wanted from you?"

"Yes," I said.

"Well, here it is. You know who Bruce Talbot is?"

"Never heard of him."

"He's Veronica MacLeish's boyfriend."

"Oh."

"You remember the other day when he parked his car in the bus lane?"

"Yes."

"And everybody was out there cheering and going crazy?"

"I remember."

"Well, it seems our friend Alfred was out there, too, and he wrote a column that makes Veronica and Bruce look pretty stupid."

"I haven't seen the paper today," I said. I didn't want him to know that I had already seen it and thought it was hilarious. Apparently, that would not have gone over too well.

"Well, they saw it and that's why I'm talking to you. Bruce wants me to find out who Alfred is. He says he wants to have a little talk with him. You ever see Bruce up close? He's a big boy. He's a welder, and welders are tough."

"What's he want to see Alfred for?"

"Guess."

"I don't know."

"He doesn't like reading about himself in the paper, especially when he's made to look like an idiot."

"He did look like an idiot."

"If I told him you said that, Winslow, you and Alfred would be in the same boat. And that's a boat you do not want to be in. Believe me."

"So what do I have to do with this?"

"What do you have to do with this? I'll tell you. You owe me a favor, right?"

"No."

"From the other day."

"I don't owe you any favors. You've never done anything for me."

Tommy walked over and put his arm around my shoulder, like he was my big brother or something.

"Harper, don't argue with me, okay? I'm under a lot of stress right now. I have a lot of things on my mind. So just cooperate, alright? You don't want to make this any worse than it already is."

"But I don't owe you ..."

"Harper," he said. He tightened his grip on my shoulder. "Just say yes, okay?"

I was starting to wince, my shoulder was hurting so bad, the big goof. I felt like taking one of the barbells and sliding it through the big hole between his ears.

"Okay," I said. "Yes. I owe you a stupid favor."

"I thought so," he said. He let go of my shoulder. "Okay, so here it is. I want you to find Alfred for me. Take your time with it. I want it to be a quiet search. We don't want him to get wind of it and go underground. Access your resources at the paper, but you cannot tell anyone what you're doing without bouncing it off me first, and you cannot let Veronica or Bruce know you're working for me. Got that? This is to be done quietly and carefully. You have one month to find him."

"If he asked you to find him, why are you asking me?"

"Because if I started snooping around, people would know something was up. Besides, you owe me one, remember?"

I stood up and started walking around the weight room. There were all these mirrors along one wall and free weights stacked on their little bars. In the middle of the room was the big universal gym with all of its pulleys and benches and weights. I walked around it about three times before I said anything.

"So you want me to find Alfred and turn him over to you, so you can turn him over to Bruce Talbot, so Bruce Talbot can turn him into a welding rod, is that it?"

"You got it," said Tommy. He had a big smile on his face.

"And I'm doing this because I owe you a favor, even though you have never done anything remotely close to a favor for me."

"Right on."

"And if I say no, you'll tell Bruce that I called him an idiot."

"No, because Bruce isn't going to know you're helping me."

"So what happens if I say no?"

"I'm sure I can think of something."

I didn't like this at all, and I'll tell you why in a minute, but first I had to find out something else.

"And what if I don't find him?"

"What?"

"What if I don't find him? What if he goes underground, as you put it, even though the only thing under this school is the furnace room? Or what if he doesn't go to this school and I can't find him? What happens then?"

The smile vanished from Tommy's face. Obviously, Bruce Talbot had been as forceful with him as he was being with me.

"You find him," said Tommy, "or we'll both be welding rods."

We finally left the weight room after we arranged that I would call him every Tuesday and Thursday at his home with progress reports, which meant my first report would be in two days, since today, being a Tuesday, didn't really count.

I had no idea how I was going to do this. For about the past year people had been trying to figure out who Alfred is, and no one had ever come close, and now I had to do it in a month with a threat of severe bodily harm hanging over my head.

Now I know what you're thinking, if nobody knows who Alfred is, how would I know if anyone has ever come close to finding him or not? Well, I'll tell you, and I'll tell you what's so funny about all of this — although maybe funny isn't quite the right word.

I know who Alfred is. It's me. I am Alfred, but if you think I'm going to tell Tommy Rowe that, then you already are a welding rod.

< 2 >

You don't believe me, do you? What's a guy like me, Harper Winslow, ex-convict, friend of a precious few and victim of jokes and pranks aplenty, what's a guy like me doing writing the most popular column in the school newspaper?

Well, at the moment, I kind of wish you were right, that it wasn't me and all I had to do now was find out who it was. But as my friend Billy from my writing class would say, "Once you've done something, you can't undo it unless you have a big enough eraser." And I don't.

It was Billy who got me into this mess in the first place. I met him last year. The first thing you should know about him is, he's not quite a hundred percent, if you know what I mean. He goes to a special school and all that, and every once in a while he has to go into the hospital to have his medication changed. But he's a fun guy to hang out with, and since I have never exactly been Mr. Popularity, I don't spend too much time looking at his weak spots. And fortunately for me, he doesn't spend much time looking at mine.

Anyway, Billy is in the same writing class that I'm in. It's called The Tuesday Cafe, in case you've heard of it, and one night we had to go out and observe something and write about it. I thought it was a pretty cool idea myself.

It was late spring so the sun was still out at around eight o'clock when everyone in the class stepped outside. We meet in a building in downtown Edmonton, so to find something to observe takes about three seconds of looking around.

I watched a guy waiting for a bus. He had on a leather jacket with tassels hanging down the arms and black leather pants and black Fry boots. He wore mirrored sunglasses and was smoking a cigarette.

I thought it was kind of funny because here was this guy, all decked out as if he was about to ride his Harley-Davidson through downtown Los Angeles or something, and he was waiting for a bus. He was probably going to pick up his bike from a friend's place or a garage somewhere, but I didn't know that for sure, and my writing teacher, his name is Josh, had told us to write down only what we knew for sure. In other words, only what we saw or heard or touched or tasted or smelled.

So I wrote about this guy on the bus and everybody thought it was hilarious. Then Billy said, "Hey, you know what? I just had an idea. This would make a great story in the newspaper. You go around and you observe people and then you write about them."

Josh didn't think it would work because a lot of people out there don't like being observed, and it might not make the publishers happy if everybody stopped buying their paper, but then he said, "But for a school newspaper, where the rules are a little bit looser, yeah, I could see something like this going over pretty well."

Now believe it or not, I write for my school newspaper, and I had just finished saying at the class before this one that I was trying to come up with a new idea for a column. Somebody asked me why and I said, "Because columnists have all the fun." I didn't know if that was true or not, but I was getting really bored with the reporting end of the business.

So that night after class I thought about Billy's idea and Josh's comments, and the next day during my spare I went to the mezzanine above the gym and watched a bunch of grade twelves play basketball. The class had been split into teams of four and the gym had been divided width-wise into three mini-courts, so there were three different games going on.

In one of the games was this team of four guys who all thought they were Michael Jordan. They had black high-tops on and every time this one guy dribbled he stuck his tongue out to his chin.

They all figured they were just about the most fantastic basketball players the world has ever known, throwing the ball around and trying all of these impossible shots, even though they never made one of them. Half the time the ball didn't even hit the backboard. It just sailed through the air and then thumped against the floor a few times before hitting the wall.

Anyway, they were playing this team made up of three guys and a girl. The girl was the only person on the team who seemed to know a thing about basketball, and she kept telling her teammates where they should stand and how to shoot.

The game lasted for fifteen minutes and the Michael Jordans lost by about 20–0. They didn't get one basket. By the time Mr. Jebson, that's the gym teacher, blew the whistle to end the game, they were all fighting and chucking the ball at each other's heads. Finally one of them took the ball and just heaved it from one end of the gym to the other, he didn't even look where he was throwing it, and the thing went right through the basket at the far end without even hitting the rim. It just went Swish!

So I wrote about this game. And early the next morning I slid my little story under the door of the newspaper room with a note to the editor attached to it. I didn't sign the note, just the column, and I slid the column under the door instead of handing it to someone later in the day because I didn't want anyone to know that I was the one doing the writing. Why? Well, for one thing, it would be pretty hard to stand back and observe people when everyone in the school knew what I was doing, and second, because it was much easier to send something in with someone else's name on it instead of my own.

Then at lunch I went back to talk to the editor, her name is Courtney Connors, about a story I was doing on the new computers the school was buying. She asked me if I knew anything about this story she had found. I said no. Then she said, "Somebody submitted this new column today. I like it. It's funny and totally unique. I don't know who wrote it, though."

"There's no name on it?" I said. I'm a lousy actor, but fortunately she wasn't looking at me.

"Oh, there is," she said, looking at the bottom of the column. I had signed it with a pencil and used my left hand so no one would recognize my handwriting, not that anyone would, but ... "I didn't see that before. It says Alfred. Who's Alfred?"

"You got me."

"We don't have any Alfreds in this school, do we?"

"Not that I know of."

"I don't think we have any Alfreds in this school. Anyway, it doesn't matter. I like it so I'm going to run it. If Alfred wants to give me another one he can, or she can. I guess it could be a girl, couldn't it?"

"Probably is a girl," I said. "She just wants to throw you. Here, let me see it."

I pretended to read it and I laughed at the end. It was all an act but she didn't notice.

I felt pretty good after she said she liked it. All of a sudden I wanted to tell her that I was Alfred and that I would be glad to write another column for her, but then somebody else walked in and she got all distracted, so I left.

The next week I slid another column under the door. This one was about a teacher who couldn't find the keys to her car. She had been carrying a big box of papers and school supplies and she had put the box on the trunk of her car so she could check her jacket pockets. Then she checked her purse. Then she started slowly retracing her steps back to the school to see if she had dropped them on the parking lot somewhere, and she was almost hit by a car full of kids heading home. Of course the driver leaned on his horn as if he was skidding out of control towards a shopping mall or something.

Then one of the guys in the back seat stuck his head out the window and said, "You know, Ms. Taylor, you should always look both ways before crossing the street." She didn't think that was particularly funny.

When she didn't find her keys on the parking lot, she returned to her car and checked all around it. She got down on her belly and looked underneath, then she bonked her head on the back fender as she was getting up. Then the slight breeze that had been blowing all day suddenly picked up and blew half of her box of papers all over the place, so she had to run around and pick all of those up.

It looked like she was just about to put her foot through the window on the driver's side when for some reason the box slid off the trunk and fell to the ground. It fell on its side so everything she had just picked up fell out again. But the first thing you could see that fell out were her car keys. I guess she had put them in the box to make it easier when she got to the car.

At the end of the column I wrote, "Maybe next time she will just leave her keys in her pocket, or leave the box at school, or look both ways before crossing the parking lot. Or maybe she'll start taking a bus to school so she won't have to worry about keys. Then again, maybe she'll stop coming to school, then she won't have anything to worry about. Come to think of it, neither will the guys in the car."

The next time I went to the newspaper room, Courtney was showing the column to her friend, Joanne.

"Isn't that funny?" Courtney was saying.

"It's hilarious," said Joanne.

"Can't you just see Ms. Taylor, all hunched over walking across the parking lot, looking for her keys, when this car comes zooming around the corner?"

"I wonder who said that to her?" said Joanne.

"Probably a grade twelve. Oh, hi, Harper," Courtney said when she saw me.

Sometimes she can be really nice and say hi and everything, and other times she can be like the Mother of Godzilla, although according to Billy, Godzilla never had a mother.

"We got another column from our friend Alfred," she went on. "And I checked it out and I found out that there hasn't been a student named Alfred enrolled in the school for the last two years at least. So we know what this person is *not* named, but that's about all."

"How's this one?" I said, trying to look as if I had ten other things on my mind, and this was the eleventh.

"Funny as the last one," she said. Then she turned back to Joanne and said, " You should have heard all the comments I got after I ran that first one. It was unbelievable! I mean, I knew it was good, but everybody just loved it. They ate it up."

I suddenly got the feeling that without a face to attach to the column, Courtney was prepared to take all of the credit for it, which is something she is very good at doing. She's always telling people why she "ran" this story or how she had to "cut" something out because it went "too far."

Sometimes I feel like saying to her, "Hey, Courtney, this ain't the *New York Times,* you know," but that would just kill her. Her favorite person in the entire world is

Anna Quindlen, the columnist at the *Times* who Courtney thinks is just the greatest.

"I already know what I'm going to put in the yearbook when I graduate," she said to me one time. "I'm going to put, under Secret Ambition, 'I want to meet Anna Quindlen in person in her office at the *New York Times*.'"

"Why don't you take off now?" is what I felt like saying to her, but I didn't. I couldn't hurt the person who gave me my first newspaper job.

I had gone to her after all of this trouble I had been in last year at the start of grade ten and told her that I wanted to write for the paper. She asked me if I had any experience and I said no, aside from this writing class I was in. She got pretty interested when I mentioned it and told me I could start the following week. I never told her that the class was for adults who were trying to learn how to write.

I didn't feel bad about not telling her that. I mean, it's not like I'm not learning anything there.

Anyway, that's how I got my column started and it has pretty well taken off since the first one. I even have my own logo now. It's a fly that looks like it's climbing up a wall. I don't know how they did it, or who did it, but it looks pretty good. The only other person who has their own logo is Jennifer Tisdale, the fashion writer, and all she has is a pair of pointy-toed shoes under her name.

Billy says he'd take a fly on a wall over pointy-toed shoes any day.

I have to say I agree with him.

< 3 >

Billy was the first person I told about my meeting with Tommy. I gave him the whole story with all the facts as I remembered them, and he said, without a moment's hesitation, "Turn yourself in."

"What?" I said. "Are you crazy? Turn myself in? This guy will eat me for breakfast if I turn myself in. I can't turn myself in. That's the absolute last thing I'm going to do."

"That's my advice. Turn yourself in."

"Your advice? What are you, my lawyer?"

"I can be."

I stood up and started to pace around his apartment. Talking to Billy can get a little frustrating at times.

"Billy, this is serious. This guy wants to turn me into a pretzel. He wants me to find me and I don't know what I'm going to do."

"Turn yourself in. We can negotiate a settlement."

See what I mean?

"Negotiate a — ?" I stopped talking for a second. All of a sudden I knew what was going on. "Billy, what kind of books are you reading right now?"

"Perry Mason," he said.

That explained it.

"That explains it then," I said.

"Explains what?" said Billy.

"This business about turning myself in and negotiating a settlement. Now I know where it's coming from."

"It's coming from right here," said Billy, pointing to his head.

"Maybe it is," I said. "But Perry Mason is putting it there."

I should probably tell you what we're talking about. Billy is a big fan of movies and books. I turned him on to the books. He was always a big fan of movies. Anyway, he is a big fan of books and ever since my brother moved away, which is like about fifteen years ago now, I have had complete access to his old book collection which consists largely of westerns and detective novels by people like Mickey Spillane and Raymond Chandler.

Now, because I have access to them, Billy has access to them. And another thing you should know about him is that he has a very creative mind. Sometimes too creative, if you ask me. Dangerously creative, if you were to ask my dad — if you could ever sit my dad down long enough to get the answer.

To give you an example, Billy and I were at the movies one time, and this guy, he was about twenty-five, cut in front of us in the lineup for popcorn. Well, I wasn't going to say anything, but Billy, fresh after reading *Trouble Is My Business* by Raymond Chandler, put his hand on the guy's shoulder and said, "End of the line, pal."

The guy turned around and looked at us. This is what he saw.

I'm about five-foot eight. I'm pretty skinny, so Dad says, every day, and I have long brown hair. Mom thinks it's long, anyway. I do not look tough, nor do I feel tough, particularly when some guy who is bigger, stronger, and older than I am is staring at me with a little smile on his face, as if he is just about to have some fun.

Billy is taller than me by a few inches and a bit heavier, but he wears glasses that have been broken about a thousand times, and he always has this totally innocent look on his face. The other thing is, whenever he's scared or excited about something, he blushes about twenty times as red as anyone I've ever seen before. It's like someone sticks a heat lamp about two inches from his face and doesn't move it until he relaxes again.

So anyway, this guy is looking at us and I'm practically shaking I'm so scared, and I look at Billy and he's already way past the color of a tomato, and the guy says, "Sorry boys, didn't know you were in line," and moves away.

I swear I was so scared that I missed the first half of the movie we went to, even though we were sitting where we always sit, third row from the front, right in the middle of the theatre.

As soon as I could talk again I said, "Billy, what did you do that for? That guy could have turned us into topping for his popcorn if he wanted to."

Billy had fully recovered by this point, of course. "No, he couldn't have," he said, stuffing about twenty red Nibs into his mouth.

"Oh, you were going to take him on, were you?"

"Trouble is my business," he said, mashing away at the Nibs. "I do what I have to do."

"Oh, right," I said. "I forgot."

When he was reading Louis L'Amor, he was always telling me to "saddle up," meaning get on my bike, and calling me an "hombre." For awhile he chewed a toothpick, until he almost choked on it.

"Billy," I said to him, to get back to our conversation. "I don't need a lawyer, alright? I'm looking for some ideas. I need a way out of this mess. Thanks anyway, though. I've heard you've got a good reputation."

I thought I'd humor him a little bit at the end there. It was nice of him to offer, plus he always gets so dejected if you totally ignore these games he likes to play.

"No problem," he said. He's a pretty easygoing guy really.

"I have to call him on Thursday night with an update."

"Tommy?"

"Yes."

"What are you going to say?"

"No idea."

We sat there in complete silence for a minute or two, then he said, "I know. Tell him you've hired a private detective."

I looked at him. He was serious again.

"A private detective," I said. I thought I should double-check.

"One of the best in the business. You had to go to the bank to pay for the guy."

"Why would I hire a private detective?"

"To show him how serious you are about finding Alfred."

"Why wouldn't I just look for him myself?"

"You did, and you came up with nothing."

"I look for two days and I can't find anything, so I hire a detective?"

"Tell him there's a woman involved."

"A woman?"

"A beautiful redhead. And an estate."

I closed my eyes and shook my head.

"Billy, I think we're getting sidetracked again."

"Tell him some old millionaire died and he left all of his money to his nephew, Alfred, because he was the only one who didn't try to kill the guy. But now everyone in the family wants to kill Alfred, so he's gone into hiding, and the only way he communicates with the outside world is through his columns."

I got up and took a walk around his little kitchen. Suddenly I had a headache. I was hungry but I was too nervous to eat anything. Billy kept going on about this redhead who offers to help Alfred, but she is really a hit woman hired by the family. Alfred falls in love with her, and she with him, and now they have to come up with a way of escaping.

He really does have an incredible mind. The best tracking dogs in the world couldn't follow this story for more than a minute.

"That's some story, Billy," I said, when he finally finished. I picked up my coat from the back of my chair and put it on. Then I sat down to put on my shoes. I was feeling really down all of a sudden. Billy is usually pretty good at helping me out, although it's not like I get put into a situation like this every day. Plus I was more scared than ever about the whole thing.

"You leaving?" he said. He seemed surprised.

"I'm going to sit downstairs and wait for my mom," I said. She was coming by in about half an hour.

"What's wrong with waiting here?"

"I need space, Billy. I need room. I can't think up here today. I feel claustrophobic all of a sudden." I did, too. It was like I had just been dropped into the world's smallest telephone booth with five other people and everyone was talking on the line at once.

"Open a window," said Billy.

"That's not going to help," I said. Then I slumped back in my chair and covered my face with my hands. Why did I have to write that stupid column in the first place? Why couldn't I have just printed off some of my mom's favorite recipes or something and handed them in?

"Want a cookie?" said Billy. He was standing in front of me, holding out a tin of cookies that looked very familiar. "They're from your house. Your mom gave them to me the last time I was there."

I took one.

"Billy, why can't we come up with an idea the way my mom comes up with a cookie recipe? We're smart people. We're creative. Why is it that every time I think of a way out of this I run into a wall?"

"I've got it," said Billy, jumping to his feet. "The redhead pretends to bump Alfred off, and the people that hired her are happy because they think they're going to get their money soon, and then she takes off with him."

This wasn't the crackerjack idea I was hoping for.

If you've ever phoned somebody to help you study for a big test, and the person you phoned knows less than you do, then you would know how I'm feeling right now.

"You want me to phone Tommy Rowe and tell him that Alfred's been bumped off?" I said. This was such a stupid idea.

"Why not?" said Billy. "It's possible."

"Come on, Billy. Some guy named Alfred, who nobody in the whole school knows anything about, writes a column about some greaseball acting like a monkey on the hood of his car, and the greaseball doesn't like it so he hires a heavyweight to find out who Alfred is, and the next thing that happens is, Alfred turns up dead? By the hand of some phantom redhead? Who is hired by some gang who wants Alfred's money? Even though no one knows who Alfred really is? And in two days, I have figured all of this out? Even though, so far as Tommy Rowe knows, I know nothing more than he does about this Alfred person? Is there anyone in this entire world who would believe a story like that?"

Billy looked pretty dejected when I finished. Sometimes, like I said, his imagination can get the better of him.

"Besides, if I said Alfred was dead, I couldn't write the column anymore."

I hadn't thought of that until now. It's kind of funny, actually. Here I am, up to my neck in soup because of the thing, but I don't want it to end. I like writing that column. It gives me an identity I've never had before, not

31

that anyone aside from Billy knows about it, but still …
it's nice to have.

At least, it was nice to have until this bounty went
out on me.

"So have him kidnapped," said Billy. "You can take
a break for a few weeks, then have him come back."

He wasn't going to let this go without a fight.

"Billy, there's not going to be a kidnapping, or an assas-
ination, or a mugging, or a hostage-taking, or a hijack-
ing, or a car chase, or a bank robbery, or anything like
that. It's too unbelievable. I doubt if Tommy would even
be able to follow it. You'd lose him in about two …"

I didn't finish my sentence. An idea had come to me
while I was talking that was too big and beautiful to ignore.
Billy was right after all! I did need legal advice. I would
hire a private detective. I might even find me a redhead.

"Billy, forgive me for everything I have just said. I
need to borrow your brain for a few hours." I was so
excited I couldn't sit anymore. I was up, pacing around
the kitchen, chomping on another cookie.

"What am I going to use?"

"Watch TV. You won't need one. Can you come over
to my place tomorrow night?"

I was on to something here, something that would
keep me healthy for at least another week, probably two,
and give me time to come up with something better.

"I guess so," said Billy.

There was a car horn honking on the street in front of
the apartment. It was my mom.

"I'll come by after school to pick you up. We'll take
the bus," I said, and I was gone.

< 4 >

When I got in the car, Mom asked me how things were with Billy and at school. Then she drifted back to whatever it was she was thinking about before she picked me up, so I thought about my idea on the way home.

I don't live in Edmonton. We — Mom, Dad, and I — live in Emville, a town about thirty-five kilometers north of the city. I have one brother and one sister, but they are both married and live with families of their own in the city. They come over quite often for visits. Too often, if you want my opinion, which no one ever does.

I get along pretty well with my parents. Their names are Benjamin and Judy. We have our ups and downs. Last year started out as a down.

In case you don't know the story, I set a fire in a school garbage can and had to go to court because of it. The judge ordered me to write an essay on how I was going to turn my life around, so I joined this writing class and spent some time with the school counsellor, Ms. Davis.

I got the essay done okay. One of the things that Ms.

Davis said I should do is talk more with my parents, so we began having these Family Days and Family Hours where we all spent time together. That lasted for about a month. Then Dad started getting really busy again, so I started writing him these little notes. That was Josh's idea. He's my writing teacher. They weren't really serious notes or anything, or I-love-you-daddy notes. Half the time they were just something stupid or funny, but he liked them and told me I should write more.

That's when I remembered my idea of writing for the school paper.

Dad is a doctor/town councillor/volunteer-a-man/ every-kid-in-town's-uncle, if you know what I mean. He likes his popularity is what I'm saying. Half the time he complains about it, and he's always talking about this imaginary little "shack" on a lake that he'd like to escape to, even though Mom doesn't even listen to him when he talks about it anymore. She says the day he moves into a shack on a lake is the day Elvis Presley plays at the Rec Center in Emville.

I think that's her way of saying that it's never going to happen.

If you want to know the truth, I don't think she wants it to happen. Mom would rather retire to a little chalet in Banff so she can ski and shop and eat a fancy dessert like a Brownie Conspiracy at Melissa's Missteak every day.

Melissa's is this restaurant Mom and Dad go to whenever they're in Banff. Dad goes to Banff on conferences all the time.

Mom runs her own clothing boutique. She used to

make all of her own clothes and then sell them in the store, but now she is too busy, so she has a corner of the store that is all her stuff, and the rest of the place has clothes made by other people. She carries no designer labels. That is the big deal with her store. No designer labels. Everything is original. She says that all the time, even to me, and I don't even shop there.

Mom and Dad and I have been getting along pretty well so far this year. Though Dad did get pretty excited when I failed a math test. He doesn't understand how anyone could fail a test in high school. Whenever he gets too upset at my grades, I say to him, "You want me to do what William did?" and he gives me this killer look and then walks away.

William is my brother. He was caught cheating on an exam in university and came this close to being tossed out. He said there was too much pressure on him and he was afraid he was going to collapse. Dad was in a state of shock for about a month. Mom kept walking around crying.

In the meantime, I had my bike stolen and when I went to the kid who took it, he punched me in the nose. So I went home with all this blood on my face, and Dad told me to watch where I'm going, and Mom told me to get the "Stain-Away" because I was wearing a new white T-shirt.

My brother is sixteen years older than I am. He is a doctor, just like Dad. My sister, Clarissa, is fourteen years older than me. She is practically a lawyer, like her husband, Mike, but they have two children and for some reason, Clarissa believes that the children benefit more from being at home with her instead of going to a daycare. I say "for some reason" because she runs her home like a daycare anyway, with nap times and "outdoor breaks" and "naughty nooks" where the kids have to go and "reflect on their misbehaviour" for a few minutes. They can never touch anything, not even in their own house. They can't even eat a cracker unless they're sitting at the kitchen table.

Even Mom and Dad think she's going a bit overboard. The last time we went to her house, Byron, my sister's son, who is now six, spilled a glass of water on the floor in the kitchen, which is linoleum, so there was absolutely no mess, and the water took about five seconds to clean up, but she still sent him to his room and told him to stay there until he was ready to be more careful.

The cool thing about Byron is, he likes going to his room. He has all of these books in there and some toys he hides under his bed.

So this time he stayed in his room for about an hour and when Clarissa went to get him for supper, he said to her, "I'm not quite ready yet, Mom. Gimme another twenty minutes."

That cracked me up. My sister walked into the living room and said, "He doesn't want to leave his room." It was like she was going to start crying or something. "He never wants to leave his room," she said.

Mom got this big "Now, now, dear" look on her face and Dad shook his head. Mike, my sister's husband, wasn't around at the time. He was working on a case at the office, even though it was about eight o'clock on a Saturday night. So I said, "Here, I'll go talk with him," and I went in and played with him for awhile. Then I said, "Hey Byron, what do you want for dessert tonight?" and he said ice cream, so I went and told my sister that Byron would come out if he could have ice cream for dessert, and she said it was too late, she had already made chocolate mousse, so I shrugged my shoulders and went back into his room. Then about ten minutes later she knocked on the door and asked what flavor he wanted, chocolate-chocolate chip, or strawberry swirl, and he was off the bed in about three seconds.

Later that night she said to me that she wasn't too crazy about bribing her son out of his room, and that the only reason she did it was to get on with the evening. So I said that the ice cream wasn't a bribe, it's just that no one ever asks him what he wants, he always gets told what he wants, and that gets frustrating after awhile.

"He's six years old, Harper. How can he know what he wants?" said my sister, who happens to know everything about everything, in case you didn't know.

"We're talking about dessert here, Sis, not real estate," I said. Then I walked away. I knew exactly what Byron was going through.

My brother has one daughter, Vanessa, who is not to be called anything but Vanessa, not Van or Nessy or anything like that, by family members or by her school friends who play with her at her house, even though she and her friends are only seven years old.

It is the kind of thing that can drive a person like me crazy, so whenever I'm alone with her, I call her anything *but* Vanessa, like Vanny or Vinny or Zsa-Zsa, and she giggles and calls me Harp the Larp.

She's really a terrific kid.

Anyway, so there I am driving home from Billy's place with Mom and we're practically in the driveway when she says to me, "So, anything new with the column?"

I just about flipped when she said that.

"Not really. Why?" I said. For all I knew, Tommy Rowe had stopped by the house on his way home from school to pass on another "message." If he did, Mom would have told him everything. She can keep a secret in her mouth for about as long as a bird can keep a worm.

"No reason. Just thought I'd ask."

"Oh," I said. I rolled down the window to get some fresh air. All of a sudden the inside of the car was like a sauna, and I was some fat guy sitting right next to the rocks who couldn't move off the bench.

"Phyllis McGill said there was quite a scene at the school the other day. Some young hot rod parked his car in the bus lane and wouldn't move or something?"

"I heard about that," I said. Phyllis McGill is one of the bus drivers. Mom and her work at the volunteer center together.

"Apparently he almost hit one of the other drivers when he left. Phyllis said she was so mad she was ready to go after him in her bus. Can you imagine that, Phyllis tearing after some little sports car with her big yellow school bus?"

"The only thing I can imagine is Phyllis tearing the big yellow wrapper off another chocolate bar," I said. I didn't like Phyllis very much. She is one of the school's larger bus drivers, and meaner. She's always throwing kids off her bus for eating even though she keeps a trough of chocolate bars and potato chips right beside her.

"That's not nice, Harper. Phyllis is a sweetheart."

"Among other things," I said.

"She said she thought it might have been Candy Talbot's son, Bruce or Bob or something. He doesn't go to your school, does he? He must be five years older than you."

"I don't know who you're talking about," I said. Of course I did, but she didn't have to know. Bruce Talbot is the guy who told Tommy to find Alfred.

"He's one to stay away from if it is. He's been alone with his mom since he was about four or five years old. I think his dad ran off with another woman or something.That was the rumor, anyway. He's been in and out of schools and detention centers. He was living in the city for awhile. I wonder what he was doing at the school?"

"No idea," I said. I was starting to feel very sick.

"I saw him the other day, now that I think of it. He was with Veronica MacLeish. You know Veronica. Pretty. Long dark hair. Her father's in construction. Very successful. I wonder what they were doing together?"

"Maybe they were running away," I said, for lack of anything better. I mean, can you believe this? Of all the things in the world that we could talk about, we had to talk about the one guy who wants to put my head in a noose, and his girlfriend who wants to yank on the other end of the rope.

"Huh," said Mom. "That would be the day. Sam MacLeish would have an absolute fit if his daughter took off with someone like Candy Talbot's son. Funny, I can't remember his name."

"I think it's Garth," I said. I hate the name Garth. I have no reason to hate it. I just do.

"No, it's not Garth. I think it's Bruce. I'll ask your father. He'll know."

"How would he know?"

"Candy Talbot is a patient of his. I don't know what for. She's a very nervous person. Always smoking. She's been in the store once or twice. Never bought anything. I don't know what she does for money. I'll have to ask your father what her son's name is."

Mom settled into a state of deep concentration after saying that, ending our little conversation about my most favorite person in the world. Now I could get on with the business of releasing the set of vise grips that had been put around my chest and tightened by Hulk Hogan.

I could barely breathe. My hands were so wet from sweat I could probably wash all the dishes in the house without going near the kitchen sink. My head hurt.

I now knew that Mom was going to start snooping around and asking questions about Bruce Talbot. I could just see it: *Oh, hello, Candy. Nice to see you in the store. Did you notice the discount rack at the front? You know, my son and I were talking about your boy the other day. What was his name again? I knew it was Bruce, I just wasn't sure. I don't know how Harper knows him. He writes for the school paper, you know. We're so proud. He even has his own column — "Fly On The Wall." I don't suppose you've seen it, have you? You should show it to Bruce sometime. He might recognize some of the names. What's he doing these days, anyway? I heard he's been out with Sam MacLeish's daughter. They'd make a lovely couple.* Blah, blah, blah ...

The next day: Ding dong. *Harper, can you get the door? Never mind. I've got it. Oh, hello, Bruce, what brings you here? Why, of course he's home. He's upstairs in his room. Why don't you just go on up and get him? Take your shoes off first, please. I just had the carpets cleaned.*

The next day: *He was so young, and so full of potential. And now this. Turned into a welding rod. What are we supposed to do with him? Benjamin can't even light a candle without burning himself.*

You think I'm joking, I know. But just watch. Mom knows everything about everybody, and if she doesn't know it, she makes it her mission to find out what it is. I wouldn't be surprised if she knows Tommy Rowe's parents as well. Wouldn't that be nice? They could all visit me in the hospital together, or carpool it to my resting place.

"Hey, Mom," I said, miraculously clearly, considering my throat was clamped shut. "Do you know Mr. and Mrs. Rowe?" I had to know. Now that I had thought about it, I had to know.

"Bill and Susan? Your friend Tommy's parents? Of course we know them. Don't be silly. We used to curl together as a foursome. Bill and your father played tennis together up until a few years ago. They were unbeatable. Bill with that big serve of his. And no one could play the baseline like your father. Susan and I used to take you kids to the playground together when you were small. Don't you remember playing with Tommy

Rowe at the playground? He was always a bit bigger than you. Not nearly as clever. I think he has an older brother and sister, too. Why, honey? Why do you ask?"

"Just wondering," I said.

I didn't feel any better or worse after hearing that. It was just something I had to know.

"It would be nice to see Tommy again. I don't think I've seen him since junior high. Do the two of you still chum together?"

Yeah, Mom, I felt like saying, we're like this.

"Not really," I said.

"The Rowes and the Talbots used to be neighbors, now that I think of it. Candy's son used to push Tommy around all the time. I think they even charged him once."

"Really?" I said. Now this was interesting.

"Oh, yes. They had an awful time. Bill used to be over at the Talbots' house practically every day. Well maybe not every day, but ..."

"What happened?"

"The Talbots moved. I think that was when Mr. Talbot ran off. I'm not sure. I don't know the whole story."

"Did Tommy ever see the guy again?"

"I don't know. I just know that Susan had a hard time just getting Tommy out the door some days, he was so scared."

I didn't ask any more questions after that. I just tried to imagine Tommy Rowe being scared of someone and I couldn't do it. He was a big kid now, and super popular. Still, I kind of felt sorry for him. I always thought he never had a worry in the world.

< 5 >

It took me about five seconds to get over my concern for Tommy Rowe. All I had to do was think about the only thing that I've been thinking about since our little chat in the weight room. It's funny, though. You would never guess by looking at him that he was ever really scared of anybody. I mean, he has all of these friends and a girl-friend, her name is Sarah. He's on the football team, even though he's just in grade eleven, and he has his own stall at the bike rack at school, which is very important.

It's like, he's one of these guys that I have always wanted to be like my whole life, and now I find out that I am like him. But not for the right reason, if you know what I mean.

It's a bit of a letdown, if you want to know the truth.

When "The Fly" really started to take off, Tommy Rowe was one of the people I imagined myself becom-ing friends with. I could see him coming up and asking me over to his house for a party or out to a movie or whatever. We would eat lunch together and hang around.

On the second Tuesday of every month, a new column would come out, and Tommy and Veronica and everybody else would read it and laugh their heads off and say things like, "Oh, man, that was great, Harper," or "You're the only person I know who could write something like that," and go on and on and on.

They would introduce me to all of the people they know from other schools as their friend "Alfred" and the whole story about my column would come out, and then these other people would want to read it, and they would like it, and so on and so on.

I would ride the school bus to football games, even though I wasn't on the team, and everybody would be saying, "Sit here, Harper. Sit here," and wherever I sat, the other people on the bus would gather around to hear if I had another story to tell.

I know all of this sounds a little bit goofy, but when you don't have many friends, and when the people around you tease you and push you around all the time, these are the types of things you think about. They're the types of things that I think about, anyway.

Of course, I never spent two minutes trying to figure out how somebody like Tommy would ever find out it was me who wrote the column. I just skipped over that little detail altogether. But that's what dreams are for, aren't they, skipping over details and things like that?

Anyway, now I'm trying to make sure he doesn't find out who I am.

Quite the turnaround, isn't it?

It's probably better this way, if you want to know what I'm thinking right now. I remember talking to Billy once about becoming popular at school, and he couldn't figure out why I would want to. He kept saying, "These people are your inspiration. If you liked them, you couldn't write about them," which was true, now that I think about it. Besides, Billy also used to say, "You don't even like football," which was something else I couldn't argue with.

But hearing that Tommy has the same fears that I do has changed everything anyway. You want to know why? Because I thought when you're popular, you're not scared of people anymore. You don't worry about things and you don't ever feel lonely. You never worry about what might happen if you go out one night to the store for a bag of potato chips and there's a gang of kids hanging around outside the door, and you never have to sit in gym class again waiting for everyone else to pick a partner before you could be paired with whoever was left. You wouldn't have to worry about any of that anymore.

But there's old Tommy, with his crewcut and ball cap on backwards, and always the coolest clothes and about fifty different pairs of shoes, and about ten people around him wherever he goes, and the most expensive mountain bike in the world, there he is walking around the hallways like some big tough guy, swiping people's lunches (mine) and taking their textbooks and stuffing them in the garbage. But the second Big Mister Bruce Talbot taps him on the shoulder and says, "Find the twerp who wrote this," he turns into a spoonful of jello and starts wobbling all over the place looking for help.

Of course, none of this helps my cause at all, does it? Whether he's made of jello or not, he's still about three times the size of me and he's still on the football team, meaning he can run fast and tackle people — not that he'd ever have to run too fast to catch me. I'm not exactly a world-class athlete, in case you were wondering.

He still has me working for him, too, if you can call what I'm doing right now work. I mean, he could have picked somebody else who would have gone tearing all over the school shouting, "Which one of you guys is Alfred? Tommy Rowe wants to know!" which would have been much easier for me to take, now that I think about it. I could have slipped a little bit lower in my chair and walked a bit slower down the hallways, just to ensure that the people who never give me the time of day anyway would be even less inclined to look at me, and after about a month or two, things would cool down.

In the meantime, I could have gone on with my column, possibly even writing about the mad search going on around me.

I think the person who wants to find me is one of those heavily muscled, shy-in-the-smarts-department football players who sees life as one gigantic pileup with a ball in the middle that he must get at all costs.

And what happens if he ever gets the ball?

He will be plastered by about twenty "brothers," each seeking the same goal, who will then be plastered themselves, by each other, and so on and so on, until one of them scores a goal or a point or whatever it's called in football, and gets a pat on the back for a job well done.

It's a simple life this pursuer of mine lives, but

if you have ever watched the football team carry on in the hallways at school or in the cafeteria, or if you have ever had the privilege of being stuck in the locker room with a few of them, you will know that anything beyond simple would be too much.

It would be like asking a cow to milk itself or a chicken to pluck its own feathers. Or maybe it would be like asking the cow to pluck the chicken, or the chicken to milk the cow. Or like asking the cow to drink a glass of milk and the chicken to eat a piece of chicken, but now we're getting into the eating and drinking thing, and that is something that football players do very well, providing they know which is which.

Good luck with your search, big man. I'll let you know if you find me.

Could you imagine the look on Tommy's face if I ever ran a column like that in the paper? He would have an absolute fit, as my mom likes to say. Mind you, under the present circumstances, it would amount to little more than a complete, tell-all confession, since I am the only one in the school who knows, outside of Tommy himself, that the search even exists.

So maybe I could write something different, like something about football players in general, or about Tommy in general, like this one time I saw him eating in the cafeteria:

Watching some people eat makes me hungry. They are so careful with their food. They sprinkle on the perfect amounts of salt and pepper and they savor each bite. They may even put their fork down at the side of their plate after each one and wash down their food with sips of water or milk. They take their time. They use a knife and fork. They chew with their mouths closed.

Watching other people eat makes me wish that I didn't need food to grow or stay healthy.

They belly up to the food line in the cafeteria and blurt their order. They don't say thanks. They start eating the second the food is put on their tray, even though they haven't paid for it yet.

When they sit at a table, they bury their heads over their food like cows grazing in a field, and they don't look up until they are done.

They are chowing down, as the saying goes, or pigging out. Stuffing their faces is another one, and they are all appropriate.

One afternoon last week I watched a student with short, short blond hair and thick shoulders and wrists eat a plate of spaghetti and french fries without a fork. He was in a hurry, possibly to get home for supper, and he had forgotten to get a fork from the silverware containers at the front of the cafeteria, so he made do with what he had — a teaspoon left on the table, and his ten fingers.

He put ketchup on his spaghetti and vinegar on his fries. He stacked spaghetti on his spoon with one hand and shoved the spoon into his mouth with the other. His plate was clear in about two minutes. Then he stood up and left.

It was quite disgusting.

As quickly as he ate his food, however, I got the feeling he thoroughly enjoyed it.

His tail was wagging as he walked out the door.

I could send that one in. He would be furious, mind you, and I am not sure what good it would do to make him even more determined to find me than he is already.

It's just that I am mad at him right now. He's let me down. Even with all of this other stuff going on and despite the fact that he has never been a friend of mine, he has let me down. And right now, I feel like getting some revenge.

Does that sound stupid? It probably does, but I don't think I care.

< 6 >

Billy didn't come over to my house Wednesday night after all. He phoned the school and left a message so I wouldn't have to ride the bus all the way into the city. He said he couldn't come over because it was Wednesday and he had ran out of soup. In Billy's world that is a very big deal, although I have no idea why.

Anyway, it was Thursday now and I was about to phone Tommy with my first update. I had my plan in place, although I would have felt a lot better about it if I had gone over it with Billy the night before.

My plan was this: I was going to try and make this search thing into a much bigger deal than Tommy ever expected in the hope that he would either call it off and make something up to tell Bruce, or become so confused that he would need at least two weeks to figure out what I said. After that, I was not sure what I would do. I had some work to do on that yet.

Here's how it went.

One ring. Two rings. Three …

"Hello." I recognized his voice right away.

"Tommy, it's Harper. I'm calling about Alfred."

I figured I would talk fast and brief and let him ask me the questions. That way I couldn't be blamed for not telling him what he wanted to know.

"Hang on," he said. I heard him tell his mom he was going upstairs to the phone in his room. A few seconds later he was on the line again

"You can hang up now," he said.

"Don't be long," said Mrs. Rowe. "I'm expecting a call from your father."

I recognized her voice right away, too. I remembered her now. She was kind of small and mousy. Nothing at all like Tommy. He must have taken after his dad, the big tennis champion. Like that's a big deal.

We were silent until we heard the click on the other end as Mrs. Rowe hung up the phone, then Tommy said, "Whaddaya got?"

Not exactly the kind of precise questioning I was hoping for.

I took a deep breath and started in with my answer. I knew this first part was going to be the most important. I had to convince him now that I knew what I was talking about.

"Well, I've talked with my lawyer — "

"Your what?" he said. You could tell he was surprised.

"My lawyer," I said. I tried to sound really matter-of-fact about it, as if calling a lawyer was as natural as brushing my teeth, which I guess it is to some people.

"Your lawyer? What do you need a lawyer for?"

"You just can't start looking for somebody without a

lawyer, Tommy," I said. D-uh.

"Why not?"

"It's against the law, for one thing."

"What is?"

"Haven't you ever heard of the Privacy Act? All citizens of this country shall have the right to privacy. Haven't you ever heard of that?" Of course I was making this up. I don't even know if there is such a thing as the Privacy Act, much less what it is.

"The Privacy Act," he said. He didn't seem too convinced.

"Besides, this guy writes for the paper, right? Haven't you ever heard of the right to free speech? Everyone has the right to say what they want without being punished for it. You've got to be careful of that. He could sue you."

"Sue me? For what?"

"Violating his rights."

"I haven't violated his rights."

"No, but you want me to."

"I never asked you to violate this guy's stupid rights. I want you to find out who he is. I just want to have a talk with him. Bruce Talbot wants to violate his rights." His voice was going up and down and all over the place. You could tell he was nervous.

"Bruce Talbot's a whole other story," I said. I was starting to feel pretty confident. Tommy was buying into this stuff a lot quicker than I'd thought he would. Thank goodness he's a football player.

"What do you mean a whole other story?"

"I mean, he's a bad egg, Tommy. He's one to stay

away from."

"How do you know?"

"I just do."

I could hear him take a deep breath over the phone. I think he was thinking about something, then he said, "So what did your lawyer say?"

"He told me to hire a private detective."

"You're kidding."

"Absolutely not. He said if I have any chance of cracking the syndicate, I'll need a private detective."

"Cracking the syndicate?" said Tommy.

"That's right."

"What's a syndicate?"

"A syndicate is an organization that Alfred writes for. He sends his column in and they distribute it to wherever it goes." I didn't know anything about syndicates myself until just a few weeks ago when Courtney, the editor at *Ragtime*, showed me this column she likes to read and said, "See, it's syndicated. The guy who writes it gets paid by 1,200 different newspapers a week." Then she said, "I keep telling you, Harper, come up with an idea for a column and you'll go places. You've got the talent."

Oh, goody, I felt like saying to her. I'll be taping Wanted posters with my face on them in her office in another week, and she's talking to me about talent.

It made me feel pretty good, actually, if you want to know the truth.

"What do you mean, 'To wherever it goes?' This guy just writes for the school paper, doesn't he?" said Tommy.

He was right into it now.

"We don't know that yet," I said. "Depends where

his syndicate is. If it's in New York or London, he could be writing for thousands of school newspapers."

"New York?"

"The Big Apple, Tommy. That's where you go if you want to get anywhere."

Like I would know anything about that. I can't even eat a big apple. I have very soft teeth. That's why my dentist drives a Porsche.

"You mean this guy doesn't even live in Emville?"

"I don't know where he lives."

"And that story may have gone into thousands of other newspapers?"

"Possibly."

"Bruce is going to go nuts." He said that more to himself than to me.

"I've got the best PI in the business working for us, Tommy. He's good. He's fresh."

"What's his name?"

"His name?" I never thought of a name for him. All the time I spent on preparation, I never once thought of giving my detective a name. "Philip," I said.

"What's his last name?"

"Uhh, that's all he goes by. Just Philip."

"You hired a detective named Philip with no last name? What kind of a deal is that?"

"I'm just going by his reputation. I don't care what his name is. He could call himself Cher if he wants to."

"Where'd you hear about him?"

I didn't cover that one either.

"My dad uses him," I said. I couldn't think of anything else.

"What's your dad need a private detective for?"

My dad is a family doctor, in case you didn't know. Family doctors do not usually have much use for private detectives.

"Investigating claims," I said. I could feel myself starting to sweat a little.

"What claims?"

"Claims. You know. Somebody comes in and says they have a sore back, my dad doesn't know if they're telling the truth or not, so he calls Philip to investigate."

"Why doesn't he just check their back?"

"Sometimes they won't let him." I was really winging it now.

"Why would they go see him if they didn't want him to check their back?"

"That's what Philip tries to find out."

"How?"

"I don't know how."

"How much does he charge?"

"I have no idea how much my dad pays him."

"I mean how much are you paying him?"

Oh, brother.

"Depends on the length of the case," I said. I have no idea what a private detective charges.

"He didn't give you a rate?"

"What's a rate?"

"Like twenty bucks an hour or fifty bucks an hour. He didn't tell you that?"

"We haven't had a chance to talk about it," I said. "He just accepted the case about five minutes before I called."

I could hear Tommy take another deep breath over the phone. I was losing him. Fast.

"He's right here if you want to talk with him," I said. It was a bit of a gamble saying that, but I had to say something because I could tell Tommy was starting to have some doubts about everything I was telling him. Besides, I was pretty sure he didn't want to talk. Tommy doesn't want anyone to know that he is involved with the search for Alfred.

"No," said Tommy.

See?

"Are you sure? You could ask him these questions yourself."

"I don't want anyone to know I'm in on this. I told you that already."

"Oh, yeah," I said. Like I had forgotten. "Well, if you change your mind ..."

"So what kind of experience does this guy have?"

"He specializes in cases involving youth," I said. "He's one of the best."

"Like what?"

"Hang on." I turned my head away from the phone and pretended to talk to Philip as if he was sitting right there beside me. "Is it okay if I tell him about some of your other cases? Why not? Oh. Okay." I went back to the phone. "He says I can't say anything because of confidentiality."

"What's that?"

"It's when you can't talk about something because it's private and confidential."

"So you have no idea what other cases this guy has worked on."

"Oh, no. He can tell me, he just doesn't want me telling you."

I was starting to wing it again. Tommy was asking some really stupid questions.

"Why not?"

"Because that's how facts get mixed up. If he says it directly to someone, everything's clear."

"Alright," said Tommy. He kind of sighed when he said it, as if he was ready to give up and just go with my plan and let me get off the phone, which was something I really wanted to do. "Let me talk to him."

My heart skipped about fifty beats.

"What?" I said. All of a sudden, I was feeling very hot.

"I said let me talk to him. If this guy's so private he's not going to go around blabbing about who he's working for. Come on. Put him on the line."

My plan was falling apart.

"He's not here anymore," I said. What else could I say? I had to think of something.

"Where is he?"

"He's downstairs. He's getting ready to go home."

"Well, go get him."

"I think he's about to leave."

"Well, stop him."

"I can't just stop him."

"What is this guy, superman? I thought he was just sitting right beside you."

"He was. Then he got up and left."

"Well, go get him. Tell him I want to talk to him."

I put the phone down. I was shaking I was so scared.

My plan, my stupid idiotic plan, was crashing down on top of me. I was paralyzed. I heard a doorbell. My heart was pounding in my ears. How could I have ever thought that I could pull this over anyone, much less someone as bright and clever as Tommy Rowe? He saw right through me. He knew there was no private detective. There was no lawyer. He was just stringing me along, waiting to make his move. Now he had made it, and I was a dead boy.

I heard someone coming up the stairs. It was Bruce Talbot with his tattooed forearms and greasy fingers, moving in for the feast. No, it was Veronica, dressed in black, mocking my funeral. The door to my bedroom opened. I could hardly breathe.

It was Billy.

"Billy?" I said. I couldn't believe it. "What are you doing here?" I had to make sure it was really him and not a mirage, or whatever those things are called that people see in the desert that aren't real.

"I came to give your mom back her cookie can. I need a refill. What's the matter with you, anyway? You look like me after gym class."

Billy is the most hopeless athlete you've ever seen in your life. Mom and Dad and I took him ice skating last winter and he pulled a pair of roller blades out of his bag and put them on, then he wiped out an entire family before they even got out of the shack where you put your skates on.

He's the only person I have ever met who has actually sunk a paddle boat. And I was there when he did it, so you have to believe me.

"Forget about what I look like, Billy. You gotta help me."

I filled him in on what was going on and how he could bail me out. I told him his name was Philip, which he didn't like, because he was now reading the Hardy Boys and could no longer relate to Mickey Spillane's Philip Marlowe.

"They are totally different people," he said. "Totally different."

I shook my head. I was now into about the fifth re-run of my life flashing before my eyes, and Billy was explaining to me the difference between Philip Marlowe and Frank and Joe Hardy.

"The Hardy Boys, they don't smoke. They don't chase women. They don't use guns."

This was too much.

"Alright, Billy, lookit. Be whoever you want to be. Be Frank, be Joe, be Chet. You can be Aunt Gertrude for all I care. But you have to get on that phone and pretend you're a private detective, alright?"

He thought about it for a second, then he said, "I'll do it."

"Thank you," I said. I felt like fainting.

"When do you want me?"

"When? Right now. I need you to do it right now. Tommy is waiting on the line."

"Can't," he said, shaking his head. "No way."

"Why not?"

"Have to catch my bus. It's pizza night at the Rec Center. If I don't go now, all the pepperoni pizza will be gone, and I won't be able to live with myself."

"You won't be able to live with yourself? What is that?" I said. He always picks the weirdest times to be dramatic.

"I believe in treating my body well," he said.

I closed my eyes and shook my head again. Where he was getting this stuff I didn't know. But what was clear was that my life was being upstaged by a piece of cold pepperoni pizza that was probably cooked in the morning and shoved under a heat lamp until someone like Billy came along to eat it.

"Billy," I said, with desperation, "I'll buy you a pizza. I'll buy you whatever size of pizza you want, with whatever toppings you want, from whatever pizza place you want, okay?"

"I'll think about it."

"Billy! This is important. Now get on the stupid phone."

I felt bad for getting mad, but how much of this was I supposed to take?

"Alright," he said.

"Let me get on the extension first," I added.

But before I went, I picked up the phone in my room and said to Tommy, "Sorry about that. He doesn't like being interrupted. I guess he has another big case he's working on. But anyway, here he is. Ask him whatever questions you want."

"I plan on it," said Tommy.

A chill ran down my back like a runaway trolley car, and I watch "The Streets of San Francisco," so I know what I'm talking about.

I gave the phone to Billy and ran to get on the extension.

< 7 >

I picked up the phone and waited for Billy to say something. After about a minute of complete silence, I put the phone down and ran back into my bedroom. I saw him standing in the middle of the room, his eyes closed, doing deep-breathing exercises, complete with knee bends and arms that fluttered out to the sides as he moved up and down.

It was a routine he had learned at one of his drama classes. It helped him concentrate.

"Billy," I said, amazingly calmly, "you're on in five seconds."

He nodded and smiled slightly, indicating first that he had heard me, and second, that he was happy to see me taking part in his little game, which to him, was not a game at all, but preparation for the biggest role, to this point anyway, of his life. Or, at least, of my life.

I ran back to Mom and Dad's bedroom and picked up the phone. A few seconds later, Billy's performance began.

His first words were, "Marlowe here. Start talkin'."

I closed my eyes. He was taking the tough-guy approach.

"Marlowe?" said Tommy. "I thought your name was Philip?"

"Take your pick," said Billy. "Philip Marlowe. I'm used to both of them."

He was using his deep, serious voice, which was actually not too bad, if you can believe it.

"Harper said you went by Philip," said Tommy.

"Harper? Who's Harper? You're talkin' to me now. And not for long, if you keep this up. Now what's the problem?"

I started to shake my head very slowly. Way to relax him, Billy, I said to myself. What are you going to tell him next, that you saw his grandmother getting a shave at the barber shop last week?

"The problem, Philip or Marlowe or whatever you call yourself, is that I told Harper two days ago that I wanted this little search of ours kept quiet, and now I find out he's gone and hired a private detective after talking with his lawyer. That doesn't sound too quiet to me."

"The only one making noise is you, kid. Now settle down. You're starting to sound like a dame I knew a few years ago. Couldn't keep her mouth shut. I had to get rid of her."

My eyes sprung open. Dame? Get rid of her? Billy?

"What'd you do?" said Tommy.

"I ditched her."

"How?"

"I switched bus routes. Instead of taking the E14 downtown, I started taking the E9 to the south side, then the LRT back over the river."

My forehead thumped against the desk I was sitting at so loudly I thought for sure Tommy heard it, but I couldn't help myself. This was now a typical performance by Billy — in character one minute, out of character the next. My only hope was that Tommy had taken enough blows to the head in football to keep him from noticing.

There was silence for a moment, then Tommy said, "So, how long have you been a detective there, Marlowe?"

"Years," said Billy.

"How many years?"

"Don't know for sure. Two. Maybe three."

"Two years?"

"That's right."

"What were you before, a cop?"

"No."

"College?"

"Guess again."

"Lawyer?"

"Come on. Don't insult me."

"What were you?"

"I worked in a mall," said Billy. "The Orange Julius near the dolphin pool at West Edmonton. I made the best chili dogs in the city."

My head was starting to hurt really badly, and it had nothing to do with hitting it on the desk.

"You mean undercover?" said Tommy.

"No. Over the counter. Just like everyone else."

"Is that a joke?" said Tommy.

"Not unless you think it's funny." said Billy.

There was silence for a minute, during which I am sure Tommy tried to figure out exactly who or what he was talking to, then he said, "So Harper tells me you've done some work with his dad."

Oh-oh.

"That's right," said Billy.

"Like what?"

"I helped him build his garage two summers ago."

Oh, no.

"I mean detective work. What kind of detective work have you done for him?"

"I don't give out that kind of information. Not to a pretty blonde with long arms, and not to you."

My head began to throb. Long legs, Billy. A blonde with long legs, not arms. Who cares how long her arms are?

"A pretty blonde with long arms?" said Tommy.

"Legs. I meant to say long legs," said Billy.

"Is this that confidentiality thing Harper was talking about?"

"No. It's got nothing to do with that. I just don't tell people anything about the cases I'm working on."

Tommy was silent for another minute, then he said, "You're kind of an oddball, aren't you, Philip?"

"Odd or even, I get the job done. That's what counts in this business."

"Yeah, well, let's hope so, pal. Tell Harper he can hire G.I. Joe for all I care, so long as he finds Alfred."

He did not sound impressed.

"Oh, I know who Alfred is," said Billy.

What?

"You do?" said Tommy.

"Been on his tail for years. The family used to live

right here in Emville. Then his father got a transfer to Brazil. Mom didn't want to go, so she took an apartment in Pittsburgh."

"Why Pittsburgh?"

"It's closer to Brazil than Emville. Shaved an hour off her flight time."

Oh, boy.

"What about Alfred?"

"Gone into hiding."

"Where?"

"I'm not sure."

"Why?"

"Nobody knows."

"How are you going to find him?"

"I have my ways."

"What are they?"

"I'm not telling."

"Why not?"

"When I find him, I'll tell you how I did it. But one of them will likely include staking out his residence."

"Do you know where he lives?"

"No."

Suddenly there was a beep on Tommy's end of the line. He put Billy on hold for a moment, then he returned and said it was his dad calling and he had to go. Then he added, "The next time you and I talk, it will be in person. You got that? I want to see you face to face."

Then he hung up.

I made a note to send a thank-you card to Mr. Rowe for calling when he did. I just have to remember not to sign it.

< 8 >

With that little endurance test finally behind us, for the moment at least, and after I popped about eight aspirins to take care of the migraine I had nesting in my head, Billy and I went out for a pizza. He ordered a medium pepperoni and zucchini with fresh tomatoes and hot peppers. I had one bite and practically spit it out of my mouth. He ate the rest.

We talked about the phone call with Tommy a little bit. Billy was very excited about his performance. I was exhausted. I couldn't even say anything except, "Uh-huh, Uh-huh, Uh-huh," the way Mom does when I'm telling her something. It actually drives me nuts when she does it because I know she's barely listening to me, so sometimes I'll throw something into my story like, "Then my teacher, Mr. Anderson, pulled this huge bottle of Scotch from his drawer and started pouring drinks for everyone."

This one time I said that, and then I stopped talking, and after about ten seconds, she stopped peeling her potatoes and looked at me and smiled and said, "Mr.

Anderson has links to Scotland? I wonder what part he's from? Go on, sweetie. I'm listening."

But anyway, Billy seemed completely unaffected by my lack of anything better to say, and just went merrily on with his review of the evening.

When he finally finished his pizza, we left the restaurant and headed for home. I walked Billy to his bus stop and waited with him until his bus arrived. Then I thanked him for coming and for helping me out, even though I wasn't sure if I should be thankful or not.

I had no idea how to react to that phone call. Part of me said, just leave it and see how much Tommy believed, while another part of me said, call him back and set the record straight.

I knew that's what Mom would say to do, if, by some freakish slip of the tongue, I told her what was going on. "It's always best to tell the truth," she would have said. But I wasn't so sure. Maybe when you're an adult honesty is always the best policy, but when you're a kid, sometimes I think it's better to review all your options.

Besides, I was running for my life. This guy, Bruce Talbot, he wanted to hurt me. And the thing was, I hadn't even really done anything. I hadn't run up to Veronica MacLeish and swiped her purse or anything like that. I had just written a little column in the paper about a guy who was acting like a fool and all of a sudden he wanted to put me on a shish kebab. Should I have turned myself in because of that? I didn't think so.

But to go along with everything Billy said was impossible. I mean, I knew my plan was to confuse Tommy and maybe the thing about the lawyer and privacy rights and all that was working and maybe it wasn't, but how could anyone believe that a woman who lived in Emville would move to Pittsburgh to be closer to her husband in Brazil? Why wouldn't she have just moved to Brazil?

Now I knew that wasn't the biggest detail in the world to be worried about. I mean, why should I have cared what Tommy thought of the woman who moved to Pittsburgh? He wasn't looking for her. But the thing was, all he had to do was ask his mom or dad one silly little question, something like, "Hey, Dad, how much closer is Pittsburgh to Brazil than Emville?" to find out that we were stringing him a line, because then his dad would say, "You actually know someone who did that?" and Tommy would tell him, and his dad would say, "I don't know, Tommy. Sounds like someone doesn't want to tell you the truth," or something like that.

That's what had me worried. If he knew we were trying to fool him, then it might not have mattered whether Bruce Talbot found me or not. Tommy Rowe would have put me in traction.

But just as I was thinking about all of that, the telephone rang again. The last thing I needed was another distraction, but I had a feeling I was going to get one.

"Hello?"

"Harper, it's Tommy. You alone?"

Oh, no.

"Kind of, yeah."

"What do you mean kind of?"

"My parents are home, but I'm alone in my room."

I was hoping I had no idea what the call was about, but my stomach told me I did.

"Good. I was just talking with my mom and dad, and they said that no one they have ever known has ever moved from Emville to Pittsburgh to be closer to someone in Brazil. And they know practically everyone who has ever lived in Emville, and they have never known anyone who has done that."

"So?" I said. It was the only word I knew I could say without stammering or blowing it completely. My entire central nervous system had gone on red alert. What was I supposed to do now — bring his parents into it? Tell him they didn't know what they were talking about? Tommy's dad, Mr. Tennis Champion, would have served me into the next century.

"So I know what you're trying to do. You're trying to confuse me, aren't you?"

All of a sudden I felt like telling him the truth.

"Tommy lookit — " I said, but he wouldn't let me finish.

"You think I'm a big moron just because I play football, don't you?"

"No, Tommy, wait."

"Well, guess what, shrimp? I'm smarter than you think. I have a lawyer, too, and I'm going to talk with him in the morning about this Privacy Act thing. And I phoned my uncle who happens to be the deputy police chief in Edmonton, and he says that he has never heard of a detective named Philip Marlowe except for some guy in a book, and he's not real."

"Okay, okay," I said.

It was time to be honest, I said to myself.

"And you know what else? I don't believe your dad

even uses a detective. I told my dad about that and he said 'No way.' Your dad would lose his license if he ever called on someone like that."

What did this guy do, tell his parents everything we talked about?

"I told my parents everything you and that friend or whatever he is said to me on the phone. They said you were mean and heartless."

Me mean and heartless?

"Did you tell them you swipe my lunch all the time and tore the pages out of my math book last year so I couldn't study for my exam?" I said. This conversation was suddenly going in a very odd direction.

"We didn't talk about that on the phone, Harper. Don't you listen?"

"Did you tell them you've gotten me to do your dirty work for some goon who doesn't even go to our school? That was the whole purpose for me phoning you, remember? Don't you think?"

I was really getting into it now. This big moron working the "poor me" angle. Forget giving him the truth. If I had a sledgehammer, I would have given him that, right across his shins.

"That's none of their business, Harper. That's between you, me, and Bruce."

"Well, don't you think any of that is a bit mean and heartless?"

"No."

"Why not?"

"Because it's not."

"Oh, that's very philosophical, Tommy."

"What?"

"Philosophical. Deep. You really thought that answer through before giving it."

"So what if I did? That doesn't mean you have to make fun of me."

"So what are you saying, you want me to apologize for what happened tonight? I didn't have anything to report so I made it up, okay? What was I supposed to do, tell you I have nothing and watch you break all my pencils tomorrow? Or is tomorrow the day you pour juice in my book bag so everything gets so sticky I can't open it?"

There. I'd come clean. Now he could shut up and get off the phone.

"You made all that up?" he said.

"Yes."

"All of it?"

"All of it."

"So you lied to me."

I took another deep breath. One more and I could fill a hot air balloon.

"I had no choice, Tommy. You're not exactly reasonable with people like me, you know."

He was quiet for a moment, then he said, "I want you to come to my counsellor's meeting tomorrow."

"Your what?"

"I see Ms. Davis every Friday, and tomorrow you're coming with me. I want you to come with me."

At the sound of the name Ms. Davis, my heart did about six cartwheels and a bungy jump off the CN Tower.

"Are you crazy?" I said.

"You're going to find out what I am."

"Those meetings are confidential, Tommy. I can't just walk in there with you." I could not go see Ms. Davis. I'll tell you why in a minute.

"That's the second time you've used that word 'confidential' on me tonight. The first time was with that bozo detective. Then he tells me he doesn't even know what the word means."

"Tommy, that wasn't a real guy. He wasn't a real detective. I told you why I had him talk to you. He just got carried away."

"He's gonna get carried away. In a body bag. So are you if you don't watch it."

"Oh, be sure and tell your parents you said that now. We're on the phone, remember."

"My parents aren't home."

"Well, tell them when they get home."

"They've gone to get me a milkshake."

"A milkshake?"

"They asked me what I wanted and I told them a milkshake. I was upset."

"What flavor?"

"Chocolate-banana."

"Ohh, those are good. Cinnamon on top?"

"No cinnamon."

"You should try it with cinnamon."

"It was chocolate-banana or strawberry-blueberry, but my mom didn't think the berries would be too fresh this time of day."

"From where?"

"Maxwell's, in the city."

"They've gone to the city to get you a milkshake because you're not feeling well after talking on the telephone?"

"I don't like being treated that way, Harper. It hurts my feelings. That's why you're coming to Ms. Davis tomorrow."

"I'm not going to Ms. Davis tomorrow."

"Yes, you are."

"No, I'm not."

"Yes, you *are*, Harper."

"No, I'm *not*, Tommy."

There was a pause, you could tell he was thinking, then he said, "Okay then. We'll do it this way. You come with me tomorrow, or I tell Bruce Talbot that you're Alfred."

The second I heard that, my entire body went numb. I was completely silent. My heart stopped beating. I could feel the hairs on the back of my neck standing at full attention.

"Don't like the sounds of that, I take it?"

Silence. I couldn't speak. My brain was spinning like car tires stuck in slush.

"I wouldn't either."

More silence. I could feel my fingers and toes start to tingle.

"So are you coming tomorrow?"

I tried to move my mouth, but all of a sudden it was like it had become someone else's mouth, and I had no control over it.

"I'll take that as a yes. We start at eleven."

I tried to talk, but still nothing came out. I tried to

wet my lips with my tongue and almost cut myself, my mouth was so dry.

"You got that, tomorrow at eleven?"

I wanted to know how he found out so fast, and what he planned on doing with me now that he knew. I could hear him starting to laugh.

"Don't worry, Winslow. I wouldn't tell Bruce you're Alfred. I don't want the real Alfred getting off the hook that easy. Besides, he'd never believe me anyway."

Click.

He was gone.

< 9 >

If you know anything about what I did last year, you'll probably know who Ms. Davis is, and why I really did not want to see her.

She is the school counsellor. I saw her twice a week for practically the whole of last year after I started that fire in the garbage can.

She is the only adult I have ever met in a school who I can honestly say that I like.

I saw her just the other day, as a matter of fact. She was looking the same as always, which means about a thousand times better than anyone else in the place. She has long, red hair down to her shoulders and these little wire-framed glasses. "They're John Lennon glasses," she said to me once.

"Who's John Lennon?" I said.

"He was one of the Beatles," she said.

I didn't know what she was talking about.

The best thing about her is her laugh. It's a real happy laugh, and she doesn't care if anyone else is laughing or not when she uses it. If she thinks something is funny, she laughs, and that's all there is to it.

You don't meet a lot of adults who act that way. Most times they check the room three times to see who else is laughing, and how hard, and when they should stop.

"Well, hello there, Harper," she said when she saw me. We met in the hallway. She stopped walking and looked right at me, as if talking to me was suddenly the most important thing she had to do. That can make a person feel pretty good, sometimes.

"Hello, Ms. Davis," I said. I don't usually say hello to people. I usually say "Hi" or "Hey" or something like that, but since she said "Hello" to me, I thought I would say "Hello" to her. "You're looking very spiffy today," I added.

That's the kind of relationship we have. I would never in a million years say "spiffy" to one of my teachers, not even to the ones who think they're real chummy with all the students, like Mr. Anderson, one of the gym teachers, who tries to come up with a nickname for everyone. Mine is "Slow," partly because of my last name, but mainly because that's the way I run. And you know these gym teachers. If you can't name the starting quarterback for the Dallas Cowboys and run the mile in under three minutes, they think there's something wrong with you.

She laughed when I said the word "spiffy." It's one that my mom always uses, and Ms. Davis buys her clothes at my mom's store, so she's probably heard her say it a thousand times.

Mom always says that customers like Ms. Davis do more for advertising her store than a full-page ad in the *New York Times* would, not that anybody from New York would actually consider for one second flying to Emville to buy a pair of pants.

"You'll have to pass that on to your mother," said Ms. Davis. "This is one of hers, you know."

"I thought I recognized it," I said. I did, too. I go to my mom's store sometimes after school and hang out until she's ready to go home. There's not much to do there, so I usually just walk around and look at all the dresses and pant suits and everything. Sometimes, when I remember, I bring a book.

"So, how are you doing?" said Ms. Davis.

"Not too bad."

"I don't see your name in the paper anymore. You're still there, aren't you?"

"Oh yeah," I said. I didn't tell her anything more than that, even though I was dying to. In fact, I was this close to telling her about my column and everything when the bell rang and she had to take off.

Now I can't believe how lucky I was.

Anyway, the reason I did not want to go see her is, Ms. Davis knows me better than anyone else in the entire world, including my parents — except my mom when a box of potato chips is missing and I'm trying to tell her that I had nothing to do with it — and I just knew that if I had to go into her office and sit in the same chair that I sat in last year, I would be singing like a bird in about two minutes, and Tommy would have the answer he was looking for.

In other words, I cannot hide anything from her. She knows when I'm upset or keeping a secret. She's not psychic or anything, she just knows who I am, and since

I am not the greatest liar in the world, she can figure out pretty quickly when things aren't adding up the way they should be.

So now my problem was, how did I get out of this thing? Tommy was practically crying on the phone. He had his parents driving all over North America to get him a milkshake, and tomorrow he was going to walk into Ms. Davis' office and tell her that I was treating him in a "mean and heartless" way, and she was going to ask me why, and all the spotlights in the world were going to be directed at my head as she waited for the answer.

I could see it plain as day, just like in the movies.

A cold, dark room, furnished with only a table and three or four of those cheap folding chairs my parents always pull out for Christmas because they don't want my brother and sister's kids spilling gravy and squishing broccoli on the good ones.

Tommy would light a cigarette and sit back coolly in his chair. Hopefully the thing would collapse and he'd burn himself on the cheek and Ms. Davis would have to rush him to the infirmary. But no, he would sit there and blow smoke rings through the still, lifeless air, and laugh at my discomfort.

"You are making this worse for yourself, Harper Winslow. Come now. Tell us what you know. We are your friends. We can protect you."

"But you're the one I need protection from."

"You musn't believe everything you hear."

"But you said it."

"You're babbling, man. Get a grip on yourself. Here, have a cigarette."

"No, thanks."

"Milkshake?"

Ms. Davis would be sitting next to me, her nose prac-tically in my face, her eyes watching my every move. She would have her notepad out and she'd be writing madly in it every time I blinked or opened my mouth.

"Tell me, Ms. Davis, what do you have there? What are you seeing?"

"He's lying, Mr. Tommy. His eyes are darting back and forth, and he is blinking frequently, sure signs of anxiety, possibly nervousness. And he is not looking at me when he speaks. He is scared."

"What about his arms? They are crossed in front of him."

"He is keeping the truth inside."

"Uncross your arms, Mr. Winslow."

"Uncross your own arms, Mr. Tommy. And quit blow-ing those stupid smoke rings in my face. They're making me sick."

"Hostility, Ms. Davis. Did you notice that?"

"I did. Directed mostly at you. He is scared of me, but angry at you."

"Tell me, Harper. Why are you angry at me?"

"Because you're an idiot."

"You know that upsets me, when you call me names."

"You asked the question. I'm just giving you the an-swer."

"Okay then. Why are you scared of Ms. Davis?"

"None of your business."

"Yes, Harper. I want to know that, too. Why are you scared of me? I thought we were friends."

"You thought wrong."

"You told me I looked spiffy the other day. That's something one friend says to another."

"I was drunk."

"You were not."

"I thought you were someone else."

"Oh, go on."

"Okay. So I said you looked spiffy. What's the big deal? What is the word 'spiffy' all of a sudden — a marriage proposal?"

"Tell me why you're scared of me, Harper."

"No."

"Is it because you cannot lie to me? You can only speak the truth?"

"No."

"Look me in the eye and say that."

"I can't."

"Then I was right. You are unable to lie to me. Now tell us who Alfred is."

"No."

"Do you know who he is?"

"No."

"Look, Mr. Tommy. He's staring right at the floor. In this case, no means yes. Who is he, Harper?"

"I don't know."

"Yes, you do. Who is Alfred? Is he a friend of yours?"

"No."

"He looked right at you when he said that."

"I can see, Mr. Tommy. Is he a relative?"

"No."

"He's looking right at you. He must be telling the truth!"

"Keep your shorts on, Mr. Tommy. Harper, is Alfred a she?"

"No."

"He's not a she, a friend, or a relative, but still you find reason to protect him. Tell me, Harper, why are you afraid to tell us who Alfred is?"

"I'm not afraid."

"Can you look up and say that?"

"Probably not."

"Then why — Omigoodness! I have the answer! I have the answer, Mr. Tommy! I know why you're afraid to tell us, Harper. Because you are Alfred! Am I correct? Are you Alfred, Harper?"

"No."

"Look at me!"

"No."

"Look at me and answer. Are you Alfred, Harper?"

Silence.

"Are you Alfred, Harper?"

Silence.

"Harper?"

"Yes. I am."

"You are Alfred."

"I am Alfred."

"You are Alfred, the Fly On The Wall."

"I am Alfred, the Fly On The Wall."

"There you go, Mr. Tommy."

"Good work, Ms. Davis."

"Thank you."

"You may go now."

"It's my office."

"That's right. It is your office. We'll be leaving now. Come along, Harper. We have a phone call to make."

Or maybe they'd turn her office into a courtroom, and Mr. Jenkins, The Oldest Living Principal In The World, would be the judge.

"Your Honor?"

"Yes, Ms. Davis?"

"I would like to call Harper Winslow to the stand."

"Very well."

"Mr. Winslow, how long have you known Mr. Tommy Rowe?"

"Too long."

"And what is the state of your current relationship?"

"Relationship?"

"Friendship then. What kind of a friendship do you have with him now? Are you close?"

"We're like this."

"Do you talk on the phone together?"

"When I have to."

"Was the conversation you had with Mr. Rowe on the telephone last night one that you quote, 'had to'?"

"Yes, it was."

"And would you share with us the nature of that conversation?"

"The nature of it?"

"What did you talk about?"

"We talked about a lot of things. Milkshakes. The Hardy Boys. My dad."

"Is that everything, or would you like me to refresh

your memory?"

"I think that's it."

"Your Honor, may I refresh Mr. Winslow's memory with a few tidbits from his conversation he had with my client last night?"

"Please do, Ms. Davis."

"Thank you, Your Honor. Now, let's see here, Harper. Where should I begin? How about a bogus interpretation of the Privacy Act, phony advice from a fictitious lawyer, wrongful use of your father's name and profession, falsely identifying a person who knows absolutely nothing about the law as a detective ... would you like me to go on, Your Honor?"

"I would like you to tell me where you're going, Ms. Davis."

"Very well. Harper, would you mind telling the court why you brought up all of these things during your conversation with Mr. Rowe?"

"I dunno."

"Come on, Harper. You can do better than that."

"They just came up. I don't know why."

"Who brought them up, Harper? Was it you, or Mr. Rowe?"

"I can't remember."

"Yes, you can."

"No, I can't."

"Ms. Davis, now may be an appropriate time to remind your witness that he is under oath."

"Thank you, Your Honor, but that won't be necessary. Harper, look me in the eye and tell me who brought up those topics of conversation."

"He did."

"Harper, you're turning all red and you're starting to scratch your arms. Now let's try this again. Who brought them up?"

"He did."

"Harper."

"Okay, I did. I brought them up. So shoot me. String me up to a tree. I brought them up."

"And why did you bring them up?"

"To confuse him, okay?"

"And why did you want to confuse Mr. Rowe?"

"So he wouldn't find out the truth."

"And what is that truth?"

"I'm not telling."

"What is that truth, Harper?"

"I told you, I'm not telling."

"Young man, you will answer Ms. Davis' question and you will do so now."

"Go easy, Your Honor. Harper, what is it you don't want to tell me?"

"That I am the person he is looking for."

"That you are Alfred, the Fly On The Wall?"

"That's right."

"You're telling me the truth?"

"You know it, Ms. Davis."

"No further questions, Your Honor."

"Thank you, Ms. Davis. That was a marvelous bit of work, if I may make such a comment."

"Thank you, Your Honor."

"Young man, you really met your match this time."

"She's a good one, Your Honor."

"She had you shaking like a cat in a dog pound."

"I didn't know cats ever went into dog pounds, sir."

"A stray cat, looking for a warm place to curl up and sleep."

"Oh. I've never seen a cat shake either, sir."

"Just imagine they do, okay, son?"

"Alright. I can do that."

"Thank you. Now let's get to that sentence."

You see what I'm getting at? Even if her little office at school stayed just the way it is, I was going to be in trouble if she got me in there.

But then I thought of another problem I had to deal with. I just remembered I had a column to write for the next day.

< 10 >

My deadline is eight o'clock every other Friday morning. That's the time I slide my column under the door of the *Ragtime* office. No one else gets there until eight-thirty, so I am always long gone by the time they see it.

I don't even ask what anyone thinks of it anymore. I really don't even hang out at the office that much. I told Courtney, the editor, that I had to cut back on the amount of time I was spending there because I was falling behind in my homework. I also told her about a month ago that I no longer wanted to be a reporter. She was a little upset at first, I think because I was the one she always gave the crummy assignments to, and now she had to find someone else.

My real reason for not going there anymore is, I don't want to say or do anything that would give me away. You know, like someone says they don't like the column for one reason or another, and I turn all red and my eyes start to water, which is how I react when someone starts tearing apart something I've done. And they ask, "What's the matter with you, Harper?" and I have to come up with something quick to say or else my cover is blown, and I'm not exactly the quickest thinker in the world.

Or someone says, "Hey, Harper, read this and tell me what you think," and I have to read my own writing and comment on it, meaning I'll have to say, "Oh man, that's hilarious," and laugh and everything, which is pretty hard to do after you've written it, because it's not like the jokes are fresh after you've spent two hours the night before writing them, or I'll say, "I don't know. It's okay, I guess," and the person will either say, "That's what I think, too" and throw my column in the garbage, or "Whaddaya mean, 'okay'? This thing is great," and I'll find myself in a massive argument about how good my own work is, with me arguing against it.

The other reason is, once I started writing my own column, everything else at the paper became really boring. I mean, you know on the evening news, they have those panels of people who talk about politics and everything. Well, my mom and dad watch the news all the time, and sometimes I sit downstairs with them, and this one night, after this super-long debate about something, Mom said, "Boy, those guys sure love to hear themselves talk, don't they?" and I could not have agreed with her more. Even Dad, who is no slouch at talking endlessly about nothing himself, nodded in agreement.

Well, that's how it was at the paper all the time. At least, that's the way I see it now. We would sit around after school with our feet up on the desks and our hands behind our heads and talk about everything from world leaders we knew nothing about to the cafeteria's Meal Of The Day, and we loved doing it because it gave us a chance to listen to ourselves. It was our reason for being there.

One of the people who was always there was this guy named Myron Talbot, a grade twelve who read the *New Yorker* magazine all the time. He used to sit by the window and smoke cigarettes until he was caught by the custodian and suspended from school for a week.

"I'm gonna write about you someday," he told the custodian, this young guy with hair halfway down his back and blue jeans with patches all over the place.

"I'm worried," the custodian said. He wasn't exactly the liveliest person I've ever seen.

"You should be," said Myron. "The world is going to know what you did to me."

He had been pretty upset with his suspension. I guess his parents hit the roof. His dad wanted him to quit the paper, but his mom said he just had to leave it for a month, which to Myron, was like his entire life.

"I really don't think the world is going to give a s —," said the custodian.

Another guy was Artie, a musician who wanted to be a folk singer. He brought his big guitar with him all the time and sat in the middle of the office with it and sang to us.

At first I thought he was the coolest guy in the world, and the only guy at the paper who really knew what was going on, but after about a month, I changed my mind. At that point I decided that he was about the most negative guy in the world, and the only guy at the paper who definitely could not sing or play the guitar, next to me, of course.

Artie only sang songs that he had written. His personal favorite was called, "This Splendid School": *We're all in this together/ This splendid school of ours/ Learning all about nothing/ Unless we move to Mars*. He was quite proud of that one. Another song was about this love affair he had once with this girl that lasted for about three days. It went, *You and me, we held hands/ Sometimes we liked to touch/ But I knew we'd never make it/ You looked around too much.*

"What does that mean?" Courtney asked him at one of our meetings. He used to sing the whole song when he got depressed, which was practically always, and when he was really depressed, he would strum his guitar and sing so loud no one else could even think.

"When there is true love, nothing else in the world exists. Two people become one, and they are the world. With Jennifer, that never happened," he said, by way of an explanation.

"You only went out for three days," said Courtney. She could get very exasperated with Artie.

"True love happens quickly. It is like lightning flashing through the sky."

"I wish a little lightning would flash through the sky right now and torch that guitar," said Tim Speers, the sports editor, who had little time for things like poetry and love, and no problem admitting it.

"Oh come on, Artie, " said Trish Johnson, the news reporter. "She probably thought you were nuts, carrying that guitar around with you all the time."

Trish was one to talk. Her boyfriend was this university guy named Simon who walked around like he was

Citizen Kane because he wrote for the university newspaper.

He even called himself a journalist. I hate people like that. They get all caught up with the fancy titles before they have any right to use them.

If that guy can call himself a journalist, then I'm an author, and I'm no author, believe me.

"This guitar is my life," said Artie, looking at the guitar on his lap the way my mom looked at my brother's son when he was a baby.

"How did you even hold hands with her? You need two hands to carry that thing," said Trish.

"We'd sit on the benches outside the school. I read her my poetry."

"Your what?"

"We walked through the trees, on bended knees/ Two warriors of love, searching for a dove."

"You actually *read* that to her?" said Trish. She had a sick look on her face, like she had eaten rotten fruit or something.

"A dove is a symbol of peace," said Artie. "We were warriors looking for peace."

"Maybe a piece of wood to club you over the head with," said Tim. "That's the only piece I'd be looking for."

Artie wrote a column called "Notes To You." It was about music, which you would think would be pretty popular in a high school, but he always reviewed bands that no one had ever heard of, and he was always super serious, so I am not sure how many people ever actually read it. I only read it a couple of times myself.

Anyway, Myron, Artie, Courtney, Tim sometimes, Trish sometimes, me, and once in awhile someone from another school, would sit around and talk, and at any particular time, any one of us could get very carried away and go on and on and on about a subject of very great and sometimes grave importance, and then we would go on and on and on some more, and probably on and on and on even more if we had the time, but we all had to get home for supper.

I brought Billy with me once. He was sleeping over, so he met me at school and we walked home together. I introduced him to everyone in the office. Billy said, "Wow, I've never been in a newsroom before," and naturally that got everyone thinking they were twice as important as they were before.

"Yup, this is where it all comes together," said Courtney, getting ready to let Billy know that she was the editor. "I've been the editor here for two years now. Getting ready to move on."

"Tell him where you're going, Court," I said. This was during the time when I was very much into all of this self-importance stuff myself, not that I'm not anymore, just not in the same way, I don't think.

"I'm thinking of going down to New York, getting on with the *Times* or something down there," she said, very nonchalantly, as if she had told us that she was thinking of going down the hall to the pop machine to get herself a Coke.

"I've been there," said Billy. "I was there two years ago. I went with my dad. I saw Mark Messier at Madison Square Garden. He was going to a hockey game."

"You saw Mark Messier?" said Tim, who could get just as excited over a sporting moment or an athlete as Artie could about looking for doves in the woods.

"Yeah. I asked him where the elephants were. He said, 'Downstairs,' and kept walking. They keep all of the animals for the circus in the basement. I didn't know that before."

"You saw Mark Messier and all you did was ask him where the stupid elephants were?" said Tim.

Mark Messier is Tim's idol. When Messier was traded from the Edmonton Oilers to the New York Rangers, Tim wore a black armband for the entire hockey season, then traded it in for a Rangers' headband, which he wore every day they had a game.

"What else was I going to do?" said Billy. He is not a hockey fan. He prefers old movies on Sunday afternoons, the circus, and David Letterman, who he really wanted to see during his stay in New York, but failed to, although he did see the theatre where Letterman does his show.

"You could have at least asked him for an autograph," said Tim, still dumbfounded by what he was hearing.

"I didn't want his autograph. I just wanted to find the elephants."

Billy also saw Madonna when he was there. She was getting out of a cab. He said she looked right at him and smiled as if she knew him.

This little tidbit prompted everyone else in the room to share their own brushes with greatness. Myron saw Mordecai Richler at a book signing once, and since Richler used to write all the time for the *New Yorker*, it was a very big deal.

"I've never even heard of the guy," said Tim, who believed that if you were not involved with sports, you were not involved with life. "Who is he?"

"He's just one of the most prolific writers this country has ever produced, that's all," said Myron, blowing his cigarette smoke into the air like he was some kind of important critic, if there is such a thing.

"Oh. Prolific. Man, that sounds important," said Tim.

"At least he doesn't run around in a jockstrap chasing other men," said Myron.

"I don't know," said Tim. "You know these prolific types. Some of them can be pretty strange."

Artie told us about seeing Bruce Springsteen in a shopping mall in Los Angeles; Courtney said she met Prince Charles when she was little and he was in Alberta for some kind of Royal Tour; Trish said she shook the Prime Minister's hand when she was in Ottawa with her family.

"Yuk," said Courtney.

"Big deal," said Tim.

"My parents made me," said Trish, even though you could tell she was excited about it.

Eventually, we got into the discussion of the day, which was the effect fame has on people, and how we would handle it should it ever come our way, or, for most of us at the time, when it does come our way.

"I don't know," said Courtney, who, if you asked her, would tell you that she was no stranger to fame as it was, being the editor of the paper and everything, and could teach us all a thing or two about life "in a fishbowl." "Some of these celebrities, they get what they deserve, you know. It's the ones who just quietly go about their business that I like."

This coming from a person whose name appears on the masthead of the newspaper. *Ragtime. The official student newspaper of the Emville Community High School. Edited by Courtney Connors.*

"I know a few athletes like that," said Tim. "A very few. Most of these kids today, the money and attention they get just go right to their heads."

Tim started calling professional athletes who are at least five years older than him "kids" after he was allowed into the press box at an Oilers game last year, and sat beside all of the reporters and columnists covering the game for the daily papers, and had his picture taken sitting in front of someone's computer. He made it look as if he was actually working on it. He even had a styrofoam cup of coffee beside him, and his sleeves were rolled up, just like the reporters in the movies.

We called him "Scoop" for awhile and teased him about how important he tried to make himself look, until one day when he got all mad and told us there was nothing funny about the big business of pro sports, and that if it wasn't for people like him, we'd all be in the dark. Then he put a cigar in his mouth, but he never actually lit it.

"Fame is fleeting," said Myron, blowing smoke rings and staring up at the ceiling. This was before he got caught by the custodian.

Myron always talked as if he was being quoted, even though, as Tim often pointed out, he never really said

– 94 –

anything. "It is brutal and vicious and it is over very quickly, and the ones who are still standing when their time is done are the ones who truly deserved it in the first place. The others are mere blips on the screen."

"You're so positive, Myron," said Courtney.

"It's true," he said. "Fame is the flower we all want in our garden, yet few of us know how to properly grow it."

"What?" said Tim.

"You know what Bob Dylan would say about this?" said Artie. Bob Dylan was his idol. I've never even heard of the guy myself, but from what Artie tells me, he's this singer from the sixties who's pretty famous.

Artie even brought in one of his CDs once (he has a Bob Dylan "collection" at home) and played it for us, but there must have been something wrong with it. Dylan sounded like he had about ten clothespins pinching the end of his nose. He couldn't sing at all.

"Bob Dylan would say, 'The answer my friends, is blowing in the wind. The answer is blowing in the wind'," said Artie, answering his own question.

"Oh, please, Artie, would you knock it off with that stuff?" said Trish.

"It's the only place to look for the answer," said Artie.

"What's the question?" said Tim.

I could go on and tell you everything they all said, but I'll just tell you instead that we talked about fame for almost two hours (Courtney eventually wrote an editorial about it), and everyone had their say about it, and some of them got very caught up with what they were saying because of course there was a visitor present, Billy, who they desperately wanted to impress, but when we were walking home and I asked Billy what he thought of everyone, all he said was, "No one asked me if I ever found the elephants."

That was all he had to say about the entire conversation.

Soon after that day, I began realizing that nothing we ever talked about at those meetings was real. Like, if someone had asked Billy about his elephants, then maybe we would have had a real discussion on animals or going to the circus with our parents or whatever, but instead, no one did, and we ended up talking about something that had nothing to do with the elephants, and really, nothing to do with us, either.

Now my column, on the other hand, is as real as this chair I am sitting on. At least, I like to think it is. Just read it. It's about me watching people do things, and then writing about it. What could be more real than that? I don't make anything up. I might change a few details once in a while, but that's just to make sure no one gets suspicious.

For example (I love talking about this stuff. Maybe this is where I become just as big a ham as those guys at the paper), there was this couple in the library one day, and they were making out like crazy, and there was this guy sitting one table over from them who couldn't help but see them, and hear them, so he started going "Ahem" really loud and coughing and then saying, "Excuse me. Pardon me. I hope I didn't bother you. I have a bit of a cold. Actually, it's more like a tickle in my throat, but…," but they just kept right on making out, so this guy kept saying "Ahem," and all that, until finally the librarian, this woman who was about two hundred years old, walked over to the guy and said, "Young man, if you can't keep quiet, I'm going to have to ask you to go outside."

The guy looked at the librarian like she's nuts and said, "Me? What about them?" and they both looked over to the couple making out, and what did they see? Two people studying so hard it looks like their brains are going to fall out right there on the table.

"What about them?" said the librarian, who obviously couldn't see the couple from where she had been sitting.

"They were tearing each other's clothes off a minute ago," the guy said. "They were all over each other. I couldn't concentrate."

The librarian looked at the couple again, who now looked like total strangers sharing a table for all the talking they were doing, and said, "Young man, I think you need a holiday. Why don't you go down to the cafeteria and buy yourself a chocolate bar?"

When I wrote about this one, I described the guy watching them as someone completely different than what he really looked like, just in case he saw me sitting at the table behind him. I kept the couple as they were, though. I knew they hadn't seen me.

The ending of this one went, "What he should do is go home and bring back a camera. Then he could prove he didn't need a holiday. Or, he could threaten to sell the pictures to their parents, and take a holiday for the rest of his life."

I do the same thing whenever I write about teachers.

Sometimes I'll make a female teacher a male, or vice versa, or I'll change the details of the situation they are in, not very much, mind you, but enough to keep any of them from thinking, "The only person I saw there was Harper. I wonder if he had anything to do with this?"

Other times I don't have to worry about it, like at this school dance I went to at the start of the year. Practically everybody at school was at the thing. That's why I didn't have to worry about writing about someone. It was one of those situations where I would be almost the last person in the place that anyone would suspect of being Alfred.

I stood by myself along one side of the gym and watched everyone dance and jump around. Some of the people were pretty good dancers and others looked like they were trying to shake something off their skin, like tiny bugs or something.

This one couple, two teachers, Mr. Cooper and Ms. Carpenter, if you want to know their names, were up there on the dance floor all the time. He is one of those guys who wears driving gloves and his shades into the school to let everyone know that he drives a cool car. He's always in the bathroom combing his hair and staring at himself and looking at how his shirt is tucked in.

Ms. Carpenter is pretty much the same, except one of the things with her is, she never says hi to anyone outside of the classroom, and the other thing is, she always walks down the hallway as if everyone else in the hallway is looking at her. You know the way people do that? It's like she thinks somebody has a television camera on her or something. She keeps her eyes straight ahead and her shoulders back and straight. She never runs or walks fast or anything. Some of the guys around here think she's pretty good-looking. She has long brown hair and she always wears really cool clothes. She's not like Ms. Davis or anything, but I guess she's okay.

Anyway, they were dancing, and you could tell they both thought they were really cool, but they are in their early thirties or so, or around that age where being cool isn't exactly what it used to be, and he's doing all of these spins and twirls and she has her hands way up in the air and she's moving her head back and forth and her hips are going all over the place, when someone bumped into her and knocked her into Mr. Cooper.

I guess her forehead must have hit his teeth because she was cut right away and he was holding his mouth. You could tell they were both in a bit of pain. She pulled a piece of kleenex out of her pocket and started dabbing at her cut, while he did these mini mouth and jaw exercises, I guess to see if he could ever eat solid foods again.

But the really funny thing about it was, they never stopped dancing. They slowed down considerably and he didn't do a single spin for about five minutes, but not for a second did they stop moving to the music. So I wrote, "Maybe they thought it was a dance marathon and if they stopped moving their feet, they would be disqualified.

"If that's the case, then they deserve a prize: his and hers stylish dance helmets, a package of Mickey Mouse band-aids, and one free trip to the dentist's chair. And if that's not enough, they can have dance lessons, as many as they want, but only offered during the day.

"That should keep them out of the classroom for awhile."

I heard someone say in the cafeteria one day that Mr. Cooper saw this in the paper and didn't like it, but that Ms. Carpenter saw it and thought it was kind of funny, which is a surprise. She walked around with a band-aid on her forehead for about a week after it happened.

I am not sure what I will write about this time. I am never completely sure until I sit down and think about it, and I have to admit, I am a little bit scared to write about someone who might put another bounty on my head.

Some people sure have a hard time laughing at themselves. That's the way Josh put it, anyway, when I was talking to him a while ago about the column. He's my writing teacher at The Tuesday Cafe. He said, "There are people out there who have a vision of themselves as one thing, and when they see or read something that is different than that vision, they get very upset. It's like thinking you're in fantastic shape, and then looking into a mirror and seeing fat everywhere."

My guess is Bruce Talbot and Veronica MacLeish saw a lot of fat when they read my column, when all along, they thought they were in pretty good shape.

Speaking of shape, maybe I'll write about Mrs. Jewel, the school secretary who never moves. She weighs about a thousand pounds and she always has an open bag of something on her desk, Smarties or Skittles or jellybeans, and the only thing I have ever seen her do is answer the telephone. Like, if you go into the office and say, "Mrs. Jewel? I'm here for Mrs. Densmore. She needs some more construction paper," then she'll say, "It's over there in the cabinet," or, "See that shelf over there? It's on that somewhere."

She's not exactly the neatest person in the world either. At Easter she had this chocolate bunny on her desk that looked more like a chocolate moose, and for about the next week, everything that came out of the principal's office had little chocolate smudge marks on it.

I was talking with her just the other day. Mom wanted a calendar of events from the school to put up in her store, so I went to ask Mrs. Jewel for a copy of one. She was eating her lunch at the time. She had something in her hand that looked like a sandwich sandwich, meaning it looked like she had an entire sandwich, with bread and everything, between two more pieces of bread, and when I walked in, she had just finished taking this humungous bite, and was not about to move or even acknowledge my existence until she was finished chewing it, which would have made me late for supper, so I reached over the counter myself and grabbed one.

That made her very upset. She said that what I had done was a violation and that I could be charged with theft, which I thought was a bit of an extreme. Then she told me to get out, so I thanked her very much for her help, and left.

Yes, I think I will write about Mrs. Jewel tonight. And tomorrow, I will go meet my maker.

< 11 >

Ms. Davis said, "Oh, well, this is a surprise," when I walked into her office.

I guess Tommy had just told her that I would be joining them this morning.

I was late getting to her office. First I had to go see the principal, Mr. Jenkins, who told me to apologize to Mrs. Jewel for "infringing on her territory the other day."

"I'm sorry I infringed on your territory the other day," I said to her. I said it purposely flat, like a telephone operator telling you there's no one answering at the other end of the line.

"You should be," said Mrs. Jewel. She had this real mean look on her face, like she woke up this morning and the tub of peanut butter she keeps beside her bed in case of an emergency was empty.

Actually, I don't know what she keeps beside her bed, but it's probably some sort of food that she can eat without using a fork.

"Don't let it happen again, Harper," said Mr. Jenkins. He could look pretty mean sometimes, too, but this time wasn't one of them. I don't think he was being mean; I just don't think he likes me very much. "We do not tolerate that sort of behaviour in this school and you know that. Now get along to wherever you're going."

Typical school stuff. No one asks for my side of the story, and nobody says thank-you to my mom for advertising the school's activities in her store, which is why I had to get the stupid calendar in the first place.

"Do you two know each other?" said Tommy. He was already in Ms. Davis' office, sitting in the chair I used to sit in.

Naturally he didn't get up when I walked in, even though it would have been polite, but that's hardly something you see very often in this place.

I'm not in a very good mood, in case you couldn't tell. I was up until about two o'clock in the morning writing my column. I kept on changing it around to make sure Mrs. Jewel wouldn't figure out it was me writing about her. (I think I'm getting paranoid.) She eventually ended up in the cafeteria reading a book by the window, which is something I've seen her do maybe once. I just wrote about the way she ate and how, when she finished, she just left her tray and all of her garbage and dirty dishes sitting there on the table, which is how she leaves her desk every night for the janitors to clean. I know because sometimes my appointments last year with Ms. Davis ended after all the office staff had gone home.

At the end of the column I wrote, *"I guess she feels that her part of the job is done. She created the mess, and now it is someone else's turn to come around and clean it up.*

"I wonder how you can get a job like that — creating mess? You must have to start pretty early in life to get good at it.

"It certainly looks to me like she did."

"We've met before, haven't we, Harper?" said Ms. Davis. She was smiling, as if she was happy to see me.

I nodded and sort of smiled back. I could feel myself starting to crack already. I also didn't like Tommy sitting in my chair. I didn't even like seeing him in her office, if you want to know the truth. Ms. Davis was my counsellor, not his.

"Have a seat, Harper," she said. "Now, Tommy, why don't you tell me what this is all about?"

Tommy told her that he had invited me to come today because he felt that my ignorance towards him and who he really is was having a negative effect on our relationship, and he wanted it cleared up.

Ms. Davis just sat there and blinked a couple of times, as if she had just heard something she had never heard before, or had never expected to hear.

I sat in my chair and tried as best as I could to not gag myself with the new pen I had in my pencil case.

He *invited* me to come today, to clear up the *ignorance* that I have towards him? Was this guy for real? And what was this about our relationship? What relationship? We didn't even have one.

"And how do you propose we do that?" said Ms. Davis, apparently recovered from the load of hogwash that Tommy had thrown in her face.

"I want him to sit here and listen," said Tommy.

"Okay," said Ms. Davis. "Let's get started then.

Where would you like to begin?"

She didn't even look at me when she was talking. I had no idea what that was about.

Tommy immediately began telling a story.

You should have heard him.

You know what he said? He said that when he was about twelve years old, he got beat up by his neighbor. He didn't say why or anything, but I got the feeling that it was because his neighbor just felt like beating someone up, and Tommy was as good a choice as anybody. Probably better, actually, because he lived right next door. The guy didn't even have to ride his bike to find him.

Anyway, this guy, this neighbor, really gave it to him. Tommy had a bleeding nose and everything, and when he ran back to his house, he was really crying.

Both of his parents were home at the time. His mother started screaming when she saw him and ran to the telephone to call her sister, Tommy's Aunt Mavis, to tell her about it. I guess they're quite close. Tommy said that anytime anything happened to anyone in the family, his mother phoned her sister Mavis.

His dad took one look at him and stormed out of the house and over to the neighbor's to have a talk with "that boy and his mother." He didn't come back for about an hour, and when he did, he never said anything. He just went into his office and slammed the door.

The point Tommy was trying to make was, with his mother on the phone and his dad over at the neighbor's house, no one was around to take care of him.

He was left completely alone, even though it was his face that had been rearranged.

So he went into the bathroom upstairs and washed the blood and everything from his nose, and then he went into his bedroom and turned on the television, and that's what he did for practically the rest of the afternoon. He sat upstairs by himself. No one came in to see how he was doing or anything.

At suppertime, his mom looked at his nose and said, "I wonder if we should get Ben to take a look at this?" meaning my dad, and Tommy's dad said, "Not on your life," and didn't even look at it or feel it to see if it was broken or anything, which gave Tommy the very clear impression that his dad was more concerned with his own reputation than about anything else. You know, like the old, "What would the guys say if they found out my kid gets beat up all the time?"

To top it off, the next day was a Monday, and when Tommy's dad walked into the kitchen and saw Tommy at the breakfast table with his school books beside him, he said, "You are not going to school, young man. Now get upstairs to your room." He was pointing his finger at him and everything.

Tommy said it was like getting grounded, which it certainly sounded like to me.

Can you imagine that, getting grounded from school?

Why don't Mom or Dad ever think of that?

Anyway, so Tommy spent the next two days at home, and when the swelling around his nose went down, he went back to school.

That was his story for the day.

When he finished, you could kind of see he had tears in his eyes. Then he started sniffing, which meant he was definitely crying.

Ms. Davis was looking at him but not saying anything. You could tell she was waiting to see if anything else was going to come out.

I just kind of sat there for a minute or two, taking in everything he had said, and then I started thinking to myself. I thought, I wonder if fish and chips is the special today in the cafeteria? Man, I hope so. I could sure go for some fish and chips. I like them best with ketchup and vinegar on the fries and a little blob of tartar sauce on the side of my plate for the fish.

I like to drink Coke with fish and chips. Fish and chips and pizza.

Coke is absolutely the only drink in the world to have with pizza, especially pepperoni pizza.

I have even run over to the store for a can of Coke with a hot pizza sitting on the kitchen table waiting for me. That's how much I like Coke with pizza.

"Thank you for sharing that with us, Tommy," said Ms. Davis, interrupting my thoughts.

"Yeah. Thanks a lot," I said.

Ms. Davis gave me a look. I don't think she liked the way I said that. But I'll tell you something, I really don't care. I mean, maybe she would have preferred it if I had jumped out of my chair and held Tommy's hand while he was talking, or hugged him when he was finished, and said, "Tommy, I think you're a worthy and capable individual, and I love you just the way you are. Now come on. Let's go get a soda."

Maybe she would have liked it if I had done that. But you know what? That was absolutely the last thing in the world I was going to do. He can cry and blubber away all he wants. I'm not going to console him. I wouldn't even share a piece of pizza with him. I'd say to him, "You're rich. Go get your own." Of course, he'd probably take mine anyway, but there's a big difference between giving someone something and having them take it.

"Is it still that way for you at home?" said Ms. Davis. She was back to looking at Tommy.

"No," he said. He had stopped crying.

"How is it now?"

"I don't get beat up anymore, so my dad doesn't ignore me anymore."

"What about your mom?"

"I guess she feels the same way."

"How do you feel about that?"

"I don't know. It's the complete opposite now. They give me all the attention in the world. The other night after I got off the phone with Harper, they could tell I was upset, so they went all over town to buy me a milkshake."

"Why the change, in your opinion?"

"Because my dad took it personally whenever I got beat up before."

"He told you that?"

"More or less."

"Is that why you beat people up, to make your dad feel better?"

"I don't know," said Tommy, but you could tell he was thinking about it.

"How do you explain the milkshake then?"

"Harper lied to me. He told me a bunch of things that weren't true and I didn't like it, so I got upset. They know I like milkshakes, so ..."

I suddenly knew what I had to say. It came to me in a flash that practically knocked me out of my chair.

"I lied to you so you wouldn't beat me up," I said.

It made such perfect sense. Of course that's why I lied to him. Ms. Davis could understand that. Who wouldn't lie in a situation like that? Just look at this guy. He's at least twice the size of me, he plays football all the time, and he's telling her that he beats people up to please his father. Who wouldn't lie to him? The guy is sick.

I can just see it now in the Rowe living room every Friday night.

"Tommy," says his dad, sitting in his favorite chair, no doubt one of those big Lazy-boy recliners, with a big pad of five dollar bills on his lap and a cigar the size of half a ring of garlic sausage plugged into his mouth. "It's allowance time, my boy. Have a seat. Now, who'd you beat up this week?"

"Uh, Harper Winslow. Tony Castleman. Benjy Singleton. Casper Loafy."

"You got a kid in your school named Casper?"

"Uh-huh. I've beat him up before."

"How hard can it be to beat up a kid named Casper?"

"It's pretty hard. He runs away all the time."

"Uh-uh. Casper don't count."

"Why not?"

"You think I'm gonna go to the club and tell the

boys how you beat up a kid named Casper? No way.
They'd laugh me out of the place. Casper don't count.
Now, who else you got here? Castleman. Singleton. Win-
slow. Winslow? Is that Benjamin's boy?"

"Yes, it is."

"Kind of a mouthy one, isn't he?"

"Sure is."

"Set fire to the school a while ago?"

"That's the one."

"I'll give you double for him. Make up for Casper."

"Thanks, Dad."

"You're welcome, son. Keep up the good work."

"I beg your pardon?" said Ms. Davis. Apparently, she hadn't been expecting me to speak.

"I said, 'That's why I lied to him.' So he wouldn't beat me up."

Now all eyes were on me.

"I never said I was going to beat you up," said Tommy.

"Oh, right," I said. "What were you going to do, help me with my homework?"

Ms. Davis held one of her hands in the air the way people do when they want silence, then she said, "Would one of you mind telling me what this is about?"

Tommy and I stopped talking and looked at each other. His look was saying to me, "Let me handle this, you little twerp." My look was saying to him, "It's all yours, Dumbo." I had no problem with that.

He took a deep, nervous breath, and started talking again, to Ms. Davis. "Harper and I have this little arrangement going, and I called him up the other night to get some information from him, and he lied to me."

Ms. Davis looked at me. "Is that how you see it, Harper?" she said.

"More or less," I said. I mean, there was obviously more to it than that, but if I said too much more, there might be a whole lot less of me as soon as we got out of her office.

"So you lied to Tommy about some information you were supposed to give him."

"I guess so. Yes."

"Because if you told him the truth, you might get beat up, is that it?"

"No," I said, very quickly. That was a little too close to the real truth for me. "I lied to him because I didn't have anything to tell him, but if I told him that, I thought he might get mad and beat me up. I wasn't hiding anything from him."

Ms. Davis thought about that for a moment, then she said, "How did the two of you enter into this arrangement. Who started it?"

"He did." We both said it at the same time, and we both pointed our fingers at each other. Ms. Davis kind of smiled. Tommy and I looked at each other.

"You told me what I had to do," I said. I couldn't believe he was trying to say that I set it up.

"You said you could help me," he said. His eyes were practically burning holes right through me.

"I did not," I said.

"You did too," he said.

"No, I never."

"Yes, you did."

"Okay, okay," said Ms. Davis. Now she had both

hands in the air.

She waited until we were both quiet and settled down, then she said, "So neither one of you wants to take the credit for setting up this arrangement. Does that mean that neither of you wants to be in it anymore?"

"I could call it quits," I said. No lying there.

Tommy started shaking his head, very slowly, from side to side. "No, you couldn't," he said.

"Why not?" said Ms. Davis.

"It's not our call. It's up to somebody else."

"Somebody else?" said Ms. Davis. "There's a third party involved with this?"

"Uh-huh," said Tommy.

"And was it this third party that set everything up?"

"Sort of," said Tommy.

"Do you have to call it a party?" I said. "It's just one guy. It's not a party."

For some reason, that was really starting to bug me, her calling Bruce Talbot a party. He's not a party. He's more like a funeral than a party.

"So you know this person?" said Ms. Davis, to me.

"I know of him," I said. Tommy gave me a little look. It was like I was getting close to some kind of sacred territory, and he was warning me not to go any closer.

"What does that mean?" said Ms. Davis. She wasn't helping me any, asking me all these questions.

"He has a reputation," I said. Tommy gave me another look. "He knows him better than I do," I said, pointing to Tommy. "Ask him."

I was getting tired of his looks.

"I don't know the guy," said Tommy. He was very

defensive about it.

"You do so, Tommy," I said. It was like, Come on, man, admit it. You know the guy better than I do.

"I do not," he said.

"You used to live right beside him," I said.

Tommy's look changed from intimidation to confusion and surprise, like he didn't know what I was talking about, or he didn't know that I knew who he was talking about when he told us his story about getting beat up.

"I'm talking about Bruce Talbot, Tommy. The guy who always beat you up when you were little. The guy who beat you up in that story you told us. The guy who has us doing this stupid search." I said it because I was mad at him for pretending he didn't know Bruce better than I did, and for setting up this stupid meeting with Ms. Davis in the first place, but after I said it, I really wished I hadn't.

We both froze as soon as it was out. Tommy looked like he had just been speared in the back. I could feel my face go completely red. Then I said, "My mom told me about you and Bruce when you were little." I don't know why I said that. I just felt I had to.

All three of us were quiet for a minute or so. Then Ms. Davis started talking about how we ought to try and remove ourselves from this situation we're in, and how hopefully, Tommy and I will become better friends when the whole thing is over.

I could have laughed out loud when she referred to Tommy and me as friends, but I didn't. I couldn't get my mind off the look on Tommy's face when I told him I knew about the history between him and Bruce. He looked so scared all of a sudden. Absolutely terrified.

And then I realized that it wasn't Bruce he was scared of. It wasn't Bruce at all.

It was his father.

Tommy didn't want to be ignored again. Or punished for getting beat up.

"Would you like Harper to come again next week?" said Ms. Davis. She was talking to Tommy.

He never really gave her an answer. He just kind of shook his head, then he picked up his book bag and walked out the door.

< 12 >

The next week was a quiet one. I didn't see Tommy once at school, and I ended up leaving messages on his answering machine on Tuesday and Thursday night.

But by Thursday I had another plan.

Billy brought his dad's video camera over on Saturday. It was one of those little, hand-held ones that you could practically carry around in your coat pocket, providing your pockets were big enough. He showed me how to use it and everything.

We shot some footage, just to make sure we were using it right. For what we had in mind, it was very important that we use the camera right.

For his "Feature Presentation," Billy pretended he was a movie star being interviewed by Mary Hart on "Entertainment Tonight".

"Well, Mary," he said, in kind of an old-man voice, like a guy whose career is over, but not because he was kicked out, but because he retired, "I'd have to say no, I never expected such high praise and glory, but then again, when I look back on my career, I say to myself, 'If not you, who else?'"

I did a reenactment of a robbery, the way you see on Crimestoppers all the time. I pretended to break into my bedroom, then I tiptoed over to my desk and began rifling through all the drawers until I found this old, half-eaten chocolate bar I'd left in there about a month ago. I don't know what made me think of the thing, but as soon as I opened one of the drawers, I started thinking about looking for it.

While I was doing this, Billy was giving a list of all the information anyone would need to identify me and turn me in. He was using the same awful voice he used the night he tried to convince Tommy that he was a detective.

"The suspect is sixteen years of age with shoulder-length brown hair, blue eyes, and no sign of any facial hair whatsoever."

I gave him a look after he said that. He knows Dad got me this shaving kit two years ago, and the thing has done nothing but collect dust ever since.

"Don't worry, honey," Mom said, the last time the topic of hair came up. "You'll be running that little razor under your nose before you know it."

"I'm not worried, Mom," I said. I meant it, too, pretty well.

"I started shaving when I was thirteen," Dad said, coming suddenly to life from behind the newspaper he had in front of his face. "Thirteen years old and I was shaving every second day."

"Oh, bravo for the big man," Mom said.

"Maybe that's why you're going bald," I said. "Your

hair supply is running out. You started growing it too soon."

"Now, Harper," said Mom.

Dad went back to reading his paper.

I guess we're all a little sensitive about hair around here.

"He weighs approximately 145 pounds and is five feet, seven inches tall," Billy continued. "He was wearing a light blue bomber jacket, a pink shirt, and tap-dancing shoes at the time of the robbery. He goes by the name of Rudolph and performs nightly at The Sands Bar and Tap-Dancing Club on 82 Avenue. His phone number at home is 444–4444. His favorite food is chicken, but a double burger from Harvey's with extra banana peppers, three slices of pickles, and a dab of mustard is his favorite meal.

"Anyone helping with the arrest of this talented young man qualifies for an award. Please call now. I'm going on holiday tomorrow morning."

"That was beautiful," I said to Billy. "You'll make a fine detective someday. Now let's replay these things to make sure we're using this camera right."

"That was acting," said Billy, pulling the videotape out of the camera. "That wasn't detective work. Detective work is when you ask people questions and write in a little notepad. That was acting. There was no detective work there."

"Okay. Acting. You'll make a fine actor someday."

We watched the videos. They were perfect. Clear. Bright. In focus. You could hear practically everything that was going on in the house, including the dishwasher downstairs when Mom put it on.

"You ready to try the real thing?" I said to Billy, after he rewound and watched his clip as an old actor talking to Mary Hart for about the tenth time.

"Yes, I am," he said.

"Let's get to work then," I said. Dad always says that. He even used it once for a campaign slogan: *Let's get to work, Emville!* He won by about a million votes, so I guess it worked, even though I got sick to death of looking at those stupid posters and placards hanging around our basement.

"Would you like one for your room?" Mom asked, after the election, holding a rolled-up poster in her hand.

"No thanks," I said. "I already have a fly swatter."

"Very funny," she said. But she didn't keep any hanging around in their room either.

My plan with Billy was this: we were going to the school to videotape someone — Billy in disguise — sliding something under the door of the *Ragtime* head office. I was then going to show Tommy the videotape and say, "See, there he is. There's Alfred. Now go get him."

I thought it would work.

I told Billy there was absolutely no talking on the thing. All he had to do was walk down a hallway, slide an envelope under the third door on the right past the boys' bathroom, and scram. He didn't have to do anything else.

Of course, I knew he would. But there's a little button on his camera that says Play, and another little button that says Stop, and I planned on pushing both of them several times during what I hoped would not be an entire day of shooting Billy walking down a hallway.

On our way to the school, he asked me questions about Alfred.

"How tall is he?"

"He's about your height."

"So I don't have to hunch my shoulders or anything? I can just walk straight up?"

"He's not an old man, Billy. He's a kid who supposedly goes to our school."

"Does he have a limp?"

"You can give him a limp if you want."

"Is he pigeon-toed or duck-footed?"

"Duck-footed? What is duck-footed?"

"You know. When your feet go like this." He put the heels of his feet together and turned his toes outward and started waddling down the street like some really lousy clown. Or a very sick duck.

"No. He's not duck-footed."

"Does he have any physical characteristics that I should try to work into my disguise, like a mustache or a tattoo or anything like that?"

I closed my eyes and shook my head and tried to imagine life with a normal friend who did not try to turn every little thing we did into a new ride at Disneyland, but I couldn't. Once Billy has entered your life, there is no way out.

"What if I said he has a tattoo? What would you do?" I said.

Billy pulled a plastic bag from out of his pocket and held it in front of my face.

"Take your pick," he said. "These are fake tattoos.

You just lick your arm, or wherever you want to put the thing, then hold it on the wet part for about two minutes, and voilà! You have a tattoo."

I looked in the bag.

"What do you have in there?" I said.

"I've got everything. Snakes. Dragons. Frogs. Spiders."

I thought about it for a minute, and then I said, "Sure. Give Alfred a tattoo. Give him a dragon right on his forearm."

In about three minutes, Billy had a tattoo on his arm of a bright green dragon breathing some pretty lame-looking flames out of his mouth.

Something for Tommy to identify Alfred with, I said to myself. Also, something to separate Alfred from me.

"Good idea," I said.

"Do I have time to do makeup? I brought everything I need from home. Blush. A buff puff."

I closed my eyes again.

"No, Billy," I said. "No makeup."

When we got to the school, we went straight to the *Ragtime* office to make sure no one was there. There wasn't. The gymnasium down the hall and around the corner was crammed with kids at a volleyball tournament, but Billy and I were completely alone.

Then we found what we figured was the best spot to set up the camera. We wanted to film from behind the action, not too far behind, but far enough so that Tommy could see a lot of Alfred, but not his face. I did not want Billy's face in the video.

"Here should be good," I said, after I tried a few

spots. I was standing in a nook that led to the room where the custodians keep all their supplies. "Now you just walk right down this hallway, slide a piece of paper under that door right there, and carry on. That's all you have to do."

I was saying this for about the hundredth time, and I wasn't sure if I was done yet.

"Do I walk fast or slow?" said Billy.

He could just about drive you crazy with his questions.

"Just walk normal," I said.

"Is he right-handed or left-handed?"

I stopped walking and looked at him.

"I have to know when I slide the paper under the door."

I didn't say anything at first, then I said, "He's right-handed."

I was being very patient, but I was doing it the way parents do when what they are really trying to say to their kids is, one more question, one more word, one more outburst of activity, and you're locked in your closet until you turn thirty.

"Okay," he said. And off we went to work.

The first take was a bust. Billy's shoelace came undone, and instead of just bending down and tying it, or ignoring the stupid thing, he looked right into the camera and mouthed, "SHOULD I TIE MY SHOE?" with extreme emphasis on every word. So we took a break while he tied his shoe, which took about fifteen minutes because it was one of those shoelaces that had been broken about fifty times and it broke again when he was tightening it, so he had to retie the whole lace before he could tie up his shoe.

The next take went fine until he slid the piece of paper that we were using as the column under the wrong door. He slid it under the second door instead of the third, so we had to track down a wire coat hanger and straighten it out and slide it under the door and very slowly pull the paper back out.

We were both lying on the floor trying to get the stupid paper with the coat hanger and all the dust and dirt and everything from peoples' shoes set off Billy's allergies. He's allergic to just about everything.

He had a sneezing fit that lasted about an hour, and naturally, neither one of us had any kleenex, so he went into the boys' washroom and sat in a stall and used toilet paper to blow his nose.

He really made a racket in there. It was amazing that no one came by to see what was going on.

When we finally got the whole video shot, we practically ran all the way back to my house. When we got there, we put the tape into the VCR and watched Billy's impersonation of me as Alfred sliding my column under the door of the *Ragtime* office.

It wasn't bad. I had to admit, it wasn't bad at all. It was far from great, but it wasn't bad.

"You done good, Billy," I said. I had this huge smile on my face.

"I'd like to do it again," he said, looking very serious. "I'm into the character now. I know Alfred better. I understand what he's thinking as he walks down the hall. What he's listening for. I want to shoot it again."

I looked at him.

"Billy, you're playing a guy who walks down a hallway and slides a piece of paper under a door. What's there to understand? Besides, I'm the guy. I know what I think about when I slide the paper under the door, and I've told you a million times, because you've asked me a million times, I'm not thinking about anything. I'm not even thinking when I do it. It doesn't take any thought."

"That's what I understand now," he said. "I'm thinking too much on the video. You can see it. I want to go back and shoot it again without thinking."

"Forget it," I said, shaking my head. Shoot it again without thinking. If you want my honest opinion, we accomplished that the first time. "We're done, Billy. I'm phoning Tommy."

I got up and started walking towards the phone in the kitchen.

"One more chance," he said. He was practically pleading with me now, so I stopped and looked over at him. He was sitting on the couch in the living room, staring at the blank television screen.

All of a sudden I felt really sorry for him.

A part of me wanted to say yes and give him another chance because I know how seriously he takes things like this, but on the other hand, a bigger part of me was saying forget it, we were lucky enough that no one saw us at school walking around with that camera, and I know Tommy goes to the gym at school every weekend to work out, and if he saw us, we'd be done.

"We can't, Billy," I said. "We can't risk it."

I didn't like saying that to him. He'd been absolutely

fantastic to me all day, bringing over the camera and everything, and I'm sure you can tell that I'm not always the greatest friend in the world to him, but something was telling me to stay clear of the school, and I was fully prepared to listen to it.

"Okay," he said, suddenly full of life and as happy as ever. "You're the director."

I rolled my eyes and continued on my way to the kitchen.

< 13 >

Tommy came over on Tuesday to watch the video.

He was his usual friendly self.

"Get me a Coke," he said as soon as I told him my parents weren't home.

"I don't think we have any," I said. Of course we did, but it's bad enough when Mom and Dad have all these people over who pour perfectly good Coke into their glasses and mix it with rye and rum or whatever. I was not about to let him have one.

"Well, check," he said. He was standing in our living room with his hands on his hips, looking around at everything. I couldn't tell if he wanted to buy the place or just tear it all down and rebuild it.

"We have Sprite. You want one of those?"

I hate Sprite. Mom likes it because it's so light and refreshing. I told her that a can of Sprite weighs just as much as a can of Coke, so how could it be light? And if you want to be refreshed, jump in a shower.

"Sure," said Tommy. That surprised me a little bit. I never thought of him as a Sprite-drinker before.

"So where's this video?" he said after I came back from the kitchen and gave him his pop. I guess it was his way of saying, "Hey, thanks, man. I owe you one."

I told him it was upstairs in my room, so we went upstairs and put on the tape. Tommy sat on the edge of the bed and got ready to watch it.

He took a swig of Sprite first, then he let out this huge belch that practically shattered the window in my bedroom.

"Nice," I said. I couldn't help myself, even though I knew that being sarcastic was not a way to get on his good side. Not that I wanted to be there anyway.

"It's the fizz," he said. "Happens all the time. Come on. Let's see this thing. I got things to do tonight."

I hit the Play button.

On came the video.

First you see an empty hallway. Then you hear foot-steps. Then suddenly a figure appears. Because I am hiding in a nook, the first thing you see is Billy's profile for about a second. Then, as he moves towards the door where he will leave his column, I step out of the nook and film him from behind. He's wearing his purple bomber jacket and blue jeans and white running shoes. He stops at the third door on the right, kneels down, slides the paper beneath the door, stands up, and walks away.

Perfect.

"That's it?" said Tommy. He had just knocked off his second power-swig of pop and I was getting ready to be blown off the bed by another belch, but magically, it never came.

"That's it," I said.

"Let me see it again."

I played it for him again.

"Man, what a geek," said Tommy, his eyes fixed on Billy sliding the paper under the door.

I looked at Tommy. I could feel myself getting all red in the face.

Billy always tells me about times when people tease him or call him names, and I've been with him when little kids have made faces behind his back. It's not that he looks any different than anyone else, but he does do some odd things once in awhile, and when his medication is off, or when he doesn't take it, he can do some very odd things. Like this one time, he took off his jacket and his shirt on a bus because he was suddenly very hot, and rode home the rest of the way topless. He's also had seizures in department stores before. But still, no one had ever said anything about him to my face until now. And here is this guy, Tommy, sitting on my bed in my bedroom drinking my pop making fun of my best friend.

"What's so geeky about him?" I said.

I know that's not exactly, "Take that back or I'll make that soda a part of your face," but I had two things to keep in mind here: one, that I am not even supposed to know who Alfred is, much less be prepared to defend him with my life, and two, in case you haven't figured this out already, Tommy Rowe is the one who can turn me into a pretzel, not the other way around.

"Look at the guy," said Tommy, pointing to the television. "Look at his clothes."

I felt better when he said that. Knocking Billy is one

thing. Knocking Billy's clothes is something different altogether. And besides, Billy is used to having people knock his clothes. I do it myself sometimes.

In fact, he came over to the house one time, and Mom answered the door, and she actually screamed when she saw him. Not a blood-curdling scream or anything like that, but a gasp loud enough for me to hear upstairs in my bedroom.

He was wearing a striped, blue and yellow T-shirt, and striped green and white pants, and the stripes on the shirt were running side-to-side, and the stripes on the pants were running up and down.

"Billy," Mom said, after she finally let him into the house. "What on earth were you thinking of when you got dressed this morning?"

Billy took about ten minutes to come up with an answer.

"I can't remember," he said. "But I haven't worn this shirt in about a month, so I put it on first, and then I couldn't make up my mind between my blue jeans or my shorts, so finally I closed my eyes and stuck my hand in my drawer and came up with these."

She didn't say anything after that, but people who get dressed in the morning by closing their eyes and wearing the first thing they come up with are not people she likes to walk down the street with, if you know what I mean. Which is why, whenever I get the chance, I bring Billy into her store with me.

"Just stand up there by the front window, Billy," I said this one time. "I'll be there in a second."

Mom practically performed laser surgery on me with

the look she gave me.

"What?" I said, pretending I didn't know.

She didn't say anything back. But I knew it was time to go.

"They are kind of funny," I said, to get back to my conversation with Tommy.

"Look at that thing on his arm. It's one of those cheap tattoo things you get at the store for like a nickel."

"I didn't even notice that," I said, leaning towards the TV. The tattoo looked awful.

"And those pants. Look at the cuffs on those pants. They go up to his knees. Man. You should take this guy to your mom's store."

"It's ladies' wear," I said.

"So what? Least she could find him something that fits."

"I'm not going to take some stranger into my mom's store and tell her to find him something that fits," I said. I wanted to remind Tommy that Alfred was a stranger, just in case he sensed my defensiveness towards him. Then I said, "Besides, maybe that's Alfred's style. He's making his own fashion statement. He doesn't care what anyone thinks."

I liked saying that. It made me feel good to point out that Billy wears what he wants and does what he wants.

"Yeah?" said Tommy, "Well, if this guy's such a lone wolf who doesn't care what other people think, why's he sneaking around empty hallways sliding pieces of paper under doors with someone else's name on them?"

My face went red again. This time a burning red, like someone had just stuck a torch in front of it.

Tommy was right, except it wasn't Billy he was right about, it was me.

All this time I've been thinking that I'm the only real person writing for the paper, that my column is real because I'm real, and I don't have to hide behind smoke rings like Myron or my guitar case like Artie or my desk with a big EDITOR sign on it like Courtney, and I don't have to act tough and cool like Tommy, even though I'm really not, when in fact I'm no more real than any of them. Maybe even less real, when you think about it. I'm hiding behind someone else's name. I've created a completely different identity for myself.

"Who knows?" I somehow managed to say. My face was so red. Fortunately for me, Tommy was trying to suck the last bits of moisture from the can of Sprite, so he wasn't looking at me.

I needed time to think so I could sort all of this out.

"How do you know that's even Alfred?" he said, lowering the can from his mouth.

"What?" I said. I barely heard him. I was sitting right beside the guy in a completely quiet house, and I barely heard him.

"How do we know that's even Alfred, if no one knows what the guy looks like or who he is? That could be some guy he has doing the drop-off for him."

"Could be," I said. My brain wasn't working at all. It was like my dad's car the time he left it at the airport for a week last winter and some kid unplugged it.

Besides, I was suddenly feeling depressed.

"How did you even know he drops off the column on Saturdays?"

"I got a tip."

"A tip. We don't even know if that was Alfred's column. That could be some guy dropping off something else at the paper."

"I don't think so," I said. I was slowly starting to come around, although I had no idea what I was coming around to. "I would have recognized him."

"How?" said Tommy. "You don't even work at the paper anymore. I checked last week."

"Yes, I do," I said. All of a sudden I was feeling like a nobody again. Nobody at school. Nobody at the paper.

"Not according to Courtney."

"Well, I do," I said. "She must have just forgotten."

"You must be an important guy if she can forget about you just like that. How many people work there — six? How can you forget someone in an office of six people? That's like somebody forgetting how many kids they have. *Oh, yeah. Joey. I forgot about him. How old is he now?* It's just like that movie, *Home Alone.* You ever see that? This family goes on a trip and forgets their kid at home and these guys try to break into the house and steal everything but the kid keeps fooling them. It's hilarious. You ever see that?"

"No, I didn't," I said. I couldn't remember if I had seen it or not.

"You should," said Tommy. "It's hilarious."

We were quiet for a minute or two after that. Then Tommy, who I am just realizing has been in an amazingly good mood since he got here, especially considering the last time I saw him was at Ms. Davis' office, where he looked like he'd eaten live worms or something, said,

"Well, that's a real fine little video you got there, Harper. Real fine. But I should probably tell you, especially since you look a little sick at the moment, that I met Veronica MacLeish at a volleyball tournament at the school on Saturday, and she told me that her and Bruce have broken up, and he's gone up north to work, and she's going out with some guy from the city now. So we're off the hook. The search is over. We don't have to find Alfred anymore."

For the second time in about three minutes, my heart stopped pumping and my brain froze.

"What?" I said.

"You got some kind of hearing difficulty?" said Tommy. "That's about the third time you've said what to me, and there hasn't been another noise in this house since I got here."

"I just can't believe what you told me," I said, which was the exact truth.

No wonder he was in such a fantastic mood. His life has been saved as much as mine has.

"I said, Bruce and Veronica are no longer going out, so we no longer have to look for Alfred. Although Veronica did say she wouldn't mind finding out who he is. Maybe I'll show her this video."

"Take it," I said. I didn't know what I was saying. I think I was delirious.

"Maybe I will," he said.

He got off the bed and pushed the Eject button on my machine and the video slid out.

"Who's Billy?" he said, staring at the cassette.

Another jolt of electricity went through me. This was

getting ridiculous.

"Who?" I said.

Tommy looked at me.

"See. You did it again. Where's your mind, man? I said, 'Who is Billy?' It says on this video, 'This tape belongs to me, Billy.' Who's Billy?"

"He's a friend of mine," I said. I had forgotten that Billy puts his name on absolutely everything.

"From school?" said Tommy.

"I met him at this writing class I go to." I didn't want to tell him any more than that. I was suddenly very tired of the whole thing.

"He lent you this tape?"

"It was his camera. The tape came with it."

Tommy was quiet for a moment, then he said, "It's not that same clown who talked to me on the phone, is it? The guy who tried to convince me he was a detective?"

"No," I said, closing my eyes. When was this visit going to end? "It's a different clown."

Tommy started to laugh. "A different clown," he said. "What did you do, join the circus?"

I didn't say anything. I knew I should have been happy, or at least relieved, but at the moment, I wasn't anything.

"You're a pretty funny guy sometimes, you know that?" he said.

I looked at him. He was serious.

"You should get back to writing at the paper. I used to read your stories. They were pretty good sometimes."

"You think so, eh?" I said. The paper was the absolute last place on earth I wanted to be at right now.

"For sure. At least I could understand what you were saying. Some of those other guys, man. That Myron guy. Whatever his name is. What is he on? I've never understood a thing the guy's said. It's like he doesn't know a single word under ten letters long."

"He likes to read his own writing," I said. Then I felt bad about saying it. At least Myron uses his own name.

We were both quiet for a minute or so after that, then Tommy, perhaps sensing my complete lack of enthusiasm towards anything he was saying, even though it was all about me, got off the bed and said, "Well, I have to run. I'll let Veronica see the tape, then I'll drop it off sometime, okay?"

He was in such a terrific mood. I don't know if I have ever been in a mood as good as his, except for maybe last year when I finished that essay I had to write.

"Hey, Tommy," I said, before he left the room. I just remembered I wanted to say something to him. "You remember the other day when we went to see Ms. Davis? I'm sorry I put you on the spot with that business about living beside Bruce when you were a kid. I didn't mean to do that."

He looked at me, then he looked at the floor and kind of smiled.

"You caught me off guard there a little bit," he said. He was still looking at the floor. "I didn't know you remembered that far back."

"I was surprised to see how scared you were," I said.

It's not the kind of thing I would normally say to someone like him, but for some reason, it seemed okay to say it.

"Yeah, well, to tell you the truth, it wasn't Bruce so much that I was afraid of," he said. He wasn't looking at me. Even when he lifted his head, he wasn't looking at me.

"Was it your dad?" I said.

"Uh-huh."

We were quiet for a few seconds, then I said, "Does it get pretty lonely around your house sometimes?"

He looked at me and kind of smiled again.

"Sure does," he said.

"I know the feeling," I said.

Neither one of us said anything after that, until he said, "Well, I'll see you around then," and moved towards the door. But just before he was out, he turned around and said, "Say hi to Alfred the next time you see him."

This time, I really thought I had a heart attack.

"Don't tell me you don't know who he is. That was the worst search ever conducted in the history of finding people."

I started to relax again. Tommy wasn't serious about finding me anymore.

My breathing slowed to the pace of a marathon runner about to collapse at the finish line.

"I tried ..." I said. I was going to say something like, "I tried my best," but I could only get the first two words out.

"You're a good friend, Harper," said Tommy. "Whoever Alfred is, he's a lucky guy."

Then he was gone for good.

< 14 >

I phoned Billy a few minutes later and told him the news, not about the last part, but just about Bruce and Veronica breaking up and the search being over.

He asked me what Tommy thought of the video, and I told him that Tommy liked the video so much he took it home with him to show Veronica.

Then I hung up and went back upstairs to write another column.

Here's how it went:

> There's this guy I know — I see him every day when I'm combing my hair — who thinks he's pretty funny.
>
> Sometimes he is pretty funny, while other times, he just thinks he's funny.
>
> He's about mid-height and has long brown hair. He wears blue jeans all the time. You almost never see him with a lighter or a book of matches anywhere.
>
> He likes to think of himself as a writer, and he's

a bit of a know-it-all, sometimes without even knowing it.

He stands to one side of the crowd all the time and writes about what everyone else is doing. He never writes any notes or anything. He just ob-serves, as he likes to say, and the rest just flows together. He got that bit from a book somewhere.

He's not as good as he thinks he is, but I sup-pose he's like everyone else in that way. The funny thing is, he never thought he was like anyone else before, but lately he has discovered some remark-able similarities between himself and other people, remarkable because he discovered them, not for what the similarities are, for they are really noth-ing new or spectacular, and now he feels it is time to come clean and let everyone know who he is.

Surprisingly, he feels very good about what he has learned. He didn't at first, but he has a brain, this person I'm talking about, and every so often, he uses it, and what he has found out is, well, I'm not sure what he's found out, but it's something. I'm pretty sure of that.

So here's your clue.

His initials, in no particular order, are WH.

And in case you didn't know, he is me.

< 15 >

I dropped that off at the *Ragtime* office about two days ago. The last I heard was, Courtney was going to turn the column into a contest and run it on the front page.

She asked me if I wanted to be one of the judges who reviews the guesses.

I said sure, why not? I'm still probably the only person in the whole school who will get it right.

The funny thing is, the judges are ineligible to play.